Finding Home

Book Six in the Boone Series

By Jim Hartsell

House Mountain Publishing

Cover by Nick Castle Design:

www.nickcastledesign.com

ISBN: 979-8-9876871-0-9

www.housemountainviews.com

Other Books by Jim Hartsell

The Boone Series:
Pushing Back
Matching Scars
Keeping Secrets
Following Frankie
Choosing Family

Other Fiction:
Tango
Rock, Paper, Scissors
Journey

Nonfiction:
Glimpses
Sisyphus and the Itsy-Bitsy Spider

Children's Books: (also available in Spanish)
Father and Sister Radish and the Rose Colored Glasses
The Box of Toys
The Boy and His Mountain
The Noise in the Woods That Doesn't Belong Here!

Chapter One

Raymond looks at me over the top of his glass. "Are you certain you have to leave? It seems you only arrived yesterday."

I nod. "We'd love to stick around, but I already put the Snake Lady off once and she wasn't all that happy about it. I got to get started on her real soon."

He turns to Molly. "You and Frankie are welcome to stay, you know."

She laughs out loud. "You're suggesting Boone leave Frankie behind? I can't even imagine that. I have to admit, though, it's tempting. You two have been great to us, just great. This has been the best two weeks I've ever had."

We're sitting out behind the main house. The little cabin where Molly and I have been staying is over on the left, and I watch Frankie come up out of the pond next to it and give herself a good shake. She sees us and starts heading our way.

Charlotte smiles. "That's wonderful to hear,

Molly. It has been our great pleasure to have you three as guests. Ray was talking about Boone on the way back from our last trip, and we were thinking of planning a trip to Tennessee when Boone called. We wanted to have a chance to visit for a little longer this time. I assume he's told you the story of how we met."

Molly nods. "The thugs in the parking lot down in Georgia. You know, Boone gives all the credit to Frankie for how that standoff ended."

Raymond gets up and goes to a little table on the edge of the patio. "That does not surprise me at all, my dear, but I maintain that it was the two of them together that stepped in and saved me from a beating, or worse." He puts a couple of ice cubes in his glass and picks up a square bottle. "Does anyone else need their drink refreshed?"

Molly and Charlotte both shake their heads, and I get up and join him at the table. I hold out my glass. "About what you give yourself." He pours, and we head back over to our seats.

When we get there Molly's gone. I look around and see her heading into the cabin with Frankie right behind her. When they're inside I say to Raymond, "I sure do appreciate you fixing up the cabin, building that ramp and doing all that other stuff before we got here. You didn't have to go to all that trouble for us."

Raymond starts to say something, but Charlotte

jumps in first. "It was a very good thing for us, Boone, to look at our house and realize that so much of it is not accessible. I'm a little embarrassed by that, and we plan to call in our architect soon to give us a sense of what we need to do. We just never thought . . . ." She looks at Raymond, and then at the big house behind us.

"I know," I say. "Before I met Molly I never thought about that stuff either. I go places now and things jump out at me I never would have even noticed before."

We're all quiet for a minute, and then Raymond says, "I know I have said this once or twice already, but it bears repeating. Your Molly is a treasure beyond price. I trust you realize that."

Charlotte nods. "The fact that you two found each other is quite remarkable."

"Yeah," I say. "Best thing that's ever happened to me."

Raymond sips his drink, sets it down, and says, "From what you told us about your trip after we parted company in Georgia, it sounds like you had quite an adventure. Would I be correct to surmise that you are now content to stay in one place, at least temporarily?"

I'm not sure what surmise means, but it sounds like a fancy way to say guess. I think about it for a minute.

"You mean, am I likely to take off again? Hit the road, just me and Frankie?"

He nods.

"I'd be worse than a fool to walk away from such a fine woman, Raymond, but you know that. We're already talking about taking another trip sometime, all three of us," I say. "One thing about this trip up to see y'all is, it's been kind of a test, you know, to see if we like traveling together."

"And?"

I look from him to Charlotte and back to him. "Hard to say if we could do a long trip, like the one I took when I ran into you. This one has been kind of short. As far as I'm concerned, though, we're good to try a longer one pretty soon. You'll have to ask Molly what she thinks."

We hear the cabin door close, and when Molly gets back she says, "I think I will have another, Raymond, if you don't mind."

We spend the rest of the afternoon there. Raymond tells their cook to bring our food outside, and we eat while the sun sets over the pond. When it starts getting dark Charlotte says, "I'm going to go inside. Molly, did you want one more look at the library before the three of you have to leave?"

"Absolutely," Molly says. "That's the best part of your house, as far as I'm concerned."

After they are inside the house I say, "She loves

that room, Raymond. I'm glad it's so easy for her to get to."

He nods.

"I'm pretty sure if she had a library like that at Sylvia's I'd never see her."

"Well, Boone," says Raymond, "I imagine you would end up visiting her if she would not come to you. It has become clear to me over the last two weeks how deeply in love the two of you are. I am very happy for you."

"It's the first time I've ever had something like this I haven't screwed up," I say. "I got to tell you, it scares me sometimes."

He laughs. "Excellent!"

I sit there with my glass in my hand trying to figure out why he's laughing at me. I'm about to start getting mad about it when he reaches over and grabs me by the arm.

"The most alive I have ever felt was when I found Charlotte, and my greatest fear was that I would do something to screw it up, as you say. I have been where you are now, Boone, although it has been some time."

He's quiet for a long time after that.

"My apologies, Boone, I was lost in memory just now," he finally says. "So, tell me about your client base. The only one you have mentioned is the Snake Lady. Are you generating other repeat customers?"

There have been a few, and when I tell him that he says, "Very good. That is the key to having a successful business. When do you think Molly will be starting to work with you?"

I don't have any idea what he's talking about. He's kind of hard to see in the light from the patio lamps, so I can't tell if he's trying to be funny or if he's serious.

"You know, there's not a lot of stuff she could help with," I say.

"That will change," he says. "Scheduling, contact with new and existing customers, record keeping, advertising, finances, taxes, all of these are most certainly within her ability. She is a very intelligent young woman, as I am sure you have noticed."

"Look, Raymond, all I'm doing is just making enough to pay the rent and stuff. I'm not thinking about turning this into any kind of business." I don't even want to think about dealing with half of the stuff he just rattled off at me.

"Of course," he says. "I was overstepping my bounds. You are right to let this be what it is for now."

I don't want to talk about this stuff, don't even want to think about it. I try to think of something to say to get him off on something else.

"How come you guys decided to live here? I mean, you've been all over the place."

He smiles. "Time to change the subject? I think that is a good idea. As you say, Charlotte and I have traveled extensively. We have seen most of the contiguous states, and when we began the task of choosing a place to build this house, the Shenandoah Valley started in the top five and eventually won out. The Appalachian Mountains are beautiful no matter what the season, and from here much of the eastern US is a day's drive away. I must say we have never regretted our choice."

I know what he means. Every time I got away from the mountains I missed them. When I tell him that he nods.

"Indeed. So, we bought this land and found an architect whose work we admired, and here we are. It is a good base of operations, and a fine place to come home to after a journey."

I think about asking him why he always sounds like he's giving some kind of speech, but he's already talking about the house and the property and I just let him run.

We talk for a while longer, about their next trip and about plans he and Charlotte have for some walking trails on the property. They've got fifty acres here, and a lot of it's in woods. I'm about to ask him what he's going to do about folks like Molly when he says, "I am considering a trail to showcase the view to the west. It is especially beautiful in the fall. I wonder if Molly would be willing to consult with us on the accessibility question."

I hear a door open and close and a minute later Molly rolls up. "Hey Molly," I say. "Raymond's got a job offer for you."

"If it's for the librarian here, I accept," says Molly with a big smile. "You and Charlotte have a wonderful collection."

I tell her about the trail plans and she turns to Raymond. "That sounds like a great idea, and I would very much like to be a part of it. Give me a little notice and I'll see if I can get Boone to drive me up here."

"Done!" says Raymond. "I am certain we can find something for Boone and Frankie to do while you are busy assisting with the western trail."

It's pretty close to midnight before we get back to the cabin and get into bed. I'm about half asleep when Molly lays her hand on my chest. "You have the nicest friends, sweetie. This has been the best vacation ever."

"Yeah, Raymond and Charlotte are good people. They've got more money than anybody else I know, but you'd never know it by the way they treat us."

"If I wouldn't miss Gram so much I'd try to talk you into finding work around here, and I would just spend all my days in the library with Charlotte. It would take me years to get through all those books."

She scoots a little closer and gives me a kiss. "Good night, sweetie."

The next morning we get the truck ready and go around to the patio. Raymond and Charlotte are there, like they are most mornings, having their first coffee of the day. There are two extra cups, and when we have ours we join them at the table.

"It is a shame you have to leave," says Charlotte. "You must come visit us again soon. When we get back from our next trip we'll let you know, and you can make plans for a return."

"Sounds good to me," says Molly.

Raymond looks at me. "My apologies for last night, Boone. I am not usually prone to dispensing unsolicited advice."

It takes me a second to remember what he's talking about. "Don't worry about it. I guarantee when I get to where I need that kind of advice you'll be the man I come to."

"Good enough," he says. "Will you be leaving right away?"

Molly's looking at me like she wants to know what we're talking about. I say, "We'd better. Don't want to get home too late, I really need to get with the Snake Lady and find out what all she wants me to do this time."

"I understand," he says. "Shall we have our breakfast out here? It is a lovely morning."

After we eat we head out to the truck and Raymond and Charlotte follow us. There are two boxes sitting on the tailgate.

"I picked out a few books I thought you might not have read yet," Charlotte says to Molly.

"And I chose not to try to compete with Gamaliel's moonshine," says Raymond. "I think you will enjoy the wines I chose for my parting gift."

I don't know what to say right now. Molly gives me a second and then says, "You didn't need to get us anything after all your hospitality, but Gram taught me it's impolite to refuse a gift. Thanks, this is awfully sweet of you." She looks over at me. "I'll let you read some of my books if you'll promise to share your wine with me."

"We'll see." I grin at her.

When we're out on the interstate Molly asks, "What was Raymond apologizing for this morning? It must have been something he said while I was in the library with Charlotte."

I tell her about his business advice and about him thinking that she would end up working with me doing office stuff. "I guess he could tell I didn't like it, him telling me how to run my life. Seems to me like things are going pretty good."

She's quiet for a few miles, and then says, "I don't think he was trying to run your life, sweetie. He's a businessman, or was before he made all that money.

It's just how he thinks."

I shrug. I know she's right, but I still didn't like it.

"Besides," she says, "I could see me working in the office."

That feels like she's taking his side, and I'm about to say something when she says, "Of course, you probably couldn't afford me. I'm not cheap, you know."

I swear, this girl, it's like she can just wave her hand and all my anger flies right out the truck window. Nothing to do but play along, I guess.

"Well, the pay wouldn't be all that good, but you'd get to work with me."

She frowns and rolls her eyes.

"And Frankie."

Frankie hears her name and takes her nose out of the window, looks over at us, and then goes back to what she was doing.

Molly laughs. "Looks like Frankie's not all that excited about working with me."

Chapter Two

I'm having a hard time settling in after our trip to Virginia. The new place is all right, but it's not as quiet as the old one and I know if I stay here until the fall I'll be able to see neighbors on three sides of me. Plus I kind of got used to having Molly with me at night. She's back at Sylvia's now, and me and Frankie come back to my place every night to sleep.

We still haven't actually done it because neither one of us wants to take a chance on her getting pregnant. I mean, we come right up to the edge of it, though, and it's really hard to hold back. The stuff she is willing to do feels awful good, and a couple of times up at Raymond's I had to get out of bed and go take a walk around the pond or something. One of those times when I got back she said, "It's a good thing you left. It's a lot harder for me to get out of bed and I'm pretty sure I wasn't going to be able to stop myself."

Sylvia didn't like it much when Molly told her she

was going with me to Virginia, but she didn't say anything to me. Just gave me a look. The second night back I get to her house a little before dinner and, when I come back in the sunroom after getting a drink of water, Molly's telling Sylvia about one of those times I had to get away from her. I don't know how much she told Sylvia about the stuff we've been doing, but when I come into the room Sylvia's face is kind of red and she won't look right at me. It takes her until halfway through dinner for her to get herself back together.

We're having dessert when she looks me straight in the eye and says, "I want to thank you for treating my Molly with so much respect. It's hard for me to hear about some of the things my little girl is doing, but I guess she's not my little girl any more."

"I won't do anything to hurt her, Sylvia," I say.

"I know."

"That's right," says Molly. "Frankie and I have an understanding. She'll chase you out of the room and down the street if I tell her to."

Sylvia can't help but laugh, "Dear, I was trying to be serious."

"I could tell," Molly says. "You don't have to worry about Boone, Gram. He is a fine man. And I promise to work on being a grown woman and your little girl all at the same time."

Now I can feel my face getting red. I'm trying to

figure out what to say when Sylvia changes the subject.

"Molly told me about the parting gifts you two received from Raymond and Charlotte," Sylvia says. "They are very generous people, aren't they?"

I nod. "You got that right. I mean, you should see their house. They've got money to burn, but they could be stingy about it and they're not. I, I mean we, haven't tried any of the wines yet that Raymond gave me, but I'll bet they're fancier than anything I'd ever get for myself."

"Maybe," says Sylvia, "we could have a dinner to celebrate something and you could provide a bottle of wine."

"A fine idea!" says Molly. "What are we celebrating?"

"I'm sure we'll think of something," Sylvia says, looking at me.

I can tell I'm supposed to say something here, but I'll be damned if I know what it is. When I look over at Molly she's turning her chair around. She heads out of the room and says over her shoulder, "I'm going to bring out the box of books Charlotte gave me. You won't believe some of the stuff that's in there."

"You need any help?" I can't wait to get out of this room. It feels real uncomfortable, and I want to ask Molly if I'm the only one feeling like that.

"I'm good," she says, and she's gone.

Sylvia says, "Sit down, Boone."

I got a bad feeling about this, but I sit down in the chair next to the kitchen.

"Over here," she says, and pats the couch next to her. "I don't want to have to shout."

I move over and she grabs hold of my hand.

"Molly's right, you know. You are a fine man," she's looking down at my hand, the one she's holding. "Have you thought about your future with her?"

Damn. I guess that's why she's holding on to me, so I won't get up and run out of the house.

Truth is, I have thought about it, enough that it scares the hell out of me. I don't want to tell Sylvia that, though. I don't want to talk about it with her at all. On the way back from Virginia I had about half decided to go see Mark, talk to him about it, see what he has to say.

I look over at Sylvia. "Is that what you were talking about, celebrating something?"

She smiles. "She's my little girl, Boone. I want her to be happy."

I'm about to say something when I hear Molly say, "Maybe I do need some help, sweetie. Can you come get this box for me?"

"Sure thing," I say. "I'll be right there."

Sylvia is still holding onto me. "Just think about it, Boone. I know you'll do the right thing sooner or later."

When I get loose from her all I can think about is getting out of there. Frankie's been watching me and when I head toward Molly's room she's right behind me, like she knows something is going on.

Molly is in the middle of the room with the box on her lap and it's about to slide off into the floor. I run over and grab it, straighten it up, and set it so it's pretty solid.

"Thanks, sweetie," she says.

"Listen, I'm going to go on home," I say.

"What's wrong?"

"Nothing. I got some stuff I, stuff I've got to do to get ready for that guy the Snake Lady gave my number to. I'm supposed to start him tomorrow."

She's looking at me like she knows I'm making this up as I go.

"I'll call you tomorrow when I get back home, let you know how it went with him," I say. "Come on, Frankie, we better get going."

On the way home I can't stop thinking about what Sylvia said to me, about doing the right thing sooner or later. It makes me think of that picture in Mark's office, and I know I need to get down to see him as soon as I can. Maybe if I make a good start on what all this guy wants me to do I can go see him in the next day or two.

My phone rings and I look at it. It's Molly, and I don't want to answer it, but I do anyway.

I can tell she's been crying.

"I was afraid you wouldn't pick up when you saw it was me," she says. "The way you ran out of here I know I've done something wrong, but I can't think of a single thing. If you'll just tell me what it was, I promise I'll never do it again," and now she's crying again.

"Listen, Molly, I . . Oh shit!!!" and I'm fighting to get the truck back on the road and Molly is screaming at me and Frankie is banging against the door and I wrestle the truck back up out of the ditch just before it would have caught the edge of the bridge support and who the hell knows what would have happened then. I get across the little bridge and pull over on the side. Frankie looks like she's okay, and I'm shaking like a damn leaf and my heart's going about a thousand miles an hour, but I think we're all right. I can still hear Molly and look around for the phone. It's in the floorboard and I pick it up.

"Listen, Molly, I got to get Frankie out and walk her around, make sure she's okay. I'll call you in just a minute," and I click off.

There's a wider place off the road just a little ways ahead and I drive to it, get Frankie out, and walk up and down the road for a minute or two. She's not limping or anything, and I know she didn't hit the dashboard or anyplace else, so I take her back to the truck. We get in, and I sit for a minute trying to get my shit back together, and then I call Molly.

There's no answer.

I'm only about ten minutes from home, so I don't try again until I'm inside. This time she picks up on the second ring.

"Hey, I tried to call a minute ago and you didn't answer."

"I was talking to Gram. What happened?"

"Front tire went into a ditch and I had to fight pretty hard to get it back on the road. We're both okay. It's dark, so I can't check the truck out. It got us home, so it's probably all right too."

Neither one of us says anything for what seems like a real long time.

Molly starts to say something but I get in there ahead of her.

"Listen, Molly, what you said about you doing something wrong, you need to stop thinking that. You didn't do anything wrong."

"I know, sweetie, and I don't think Gram and I are done talking about this. She told me what she said to you while I was gone getting the books, and she can't do stuff like—"

I jump in before she gets done talking. "Not her fault, or yours either. I'm the one who ran off like a little kid. I'm not proud of that, darlin', but I can't take it back. Wish I could."

"I wish you were still here," she says. "Guess it's

too late for you to come back?"

"I better stay here and get ready for tomorrow. I'll call you after work."

"Okay. And, Boone," she says after a second, "I would never push you into anything you didn't want to do. You know that, right?"

I hate doing this kind of stuff over the phone. It's hard enough in person. I'm no good at talking to people, and the phone just makes it worse.

"I know, and it's not that I don't want, I mean, it's not . . . . Listen, can we talk about this next time I come over?"

"Sure," she says, and I can't tell if she likes that or hates it.

The job I start the next day is going to take at least three days, maybe more. The guy has about ten acres and there's a little barn not too far from his garage that he wants to start using. It's been so long since anybody's been using it I've got to cut away a bunch of brush just to get the truck back to it, and it's full of old furniture and stuff like that. He wants to have a look before I throw anything away, so I tell him I'll get him to come look at each load before I haul it off.

He seems like a nice enough guy, and half way through the first afternoon I get a track cut back to the barn door and tell him I'll start cleaning it out in the morning. He's good with that, and I call Mark and tell him I need to talk to him. The next afternoon me and Frankie are sitting in his office.

When I finish telling Mark about my talk with Sylvia, he grins at me.

"What's so funny?"

"It's not that anything is funny, Boone. I'm just really happy for you," says Mark.

I don't know what the hell he's talking about right now. My talk with Sylvia wasn't a happy talk. Felt pretty tense to me, and I tell him that.

"Oh, I don't doubt it was an uncomfortable situation for both of you," says Mark. "It was especially hard for you, because you've been so on your own for several years now. I'm happy for you because this is the kind of conversation that happens in families. You notice Sylvia didn't tell you to stay away or even slow down in your relationship with Molly? It sounds like she already thinks of you as part of the family, and for someone in her position, and of her generation, there is another step in your relationship with Molly that I believe she hopes you will take."

I'm trying to think my way through all that and Mark puts his elbows on his desk and leans toward me. "This isn't just part of being a grown man, Boone. It's part of being human. We exist in families, and if we don't have one, we look for one. It is your great good fortune to have stumbled into such a fine family as Sylvia and Molly have made, and they are welcoming you in. I know it's not what Sylvia was talking about, but if that isn't a cause for celebration I don't know what is."

I point to the picture on his wall.

"What she said about me doing the right thing made me think about that picture," I say, "and I'll be damned if I know what the right thing is right now. I think about this stuff and I feel like a little kid. I'm scared, man."

We look up at the picture. There are three more people stuck in between the frame and the glass along with me and Frankie.

"I hope you didn't get the idea from me telling you about this gift, and all those fine folks, that doing the right thing is an easy way to go. It's not. Sometimes it takes real courage, and sometimes it's scary as hell." He smiles when I look up. "Just because I don't often use that kind of language doesn't mean I don't know how to."

"I'm kind of glad you did. You were getting kind of preachy there, and scary as hell sure took the edge off of that."

He laughs. "Okay, Boone, I'll try to restrain myself. Did I ever tell you one of the reasons I look forward to your visits is that I get so many good sermon ideas from talking to you?"

He holds up his hand when he sees the look on my

face. "Don't worry, I don't preach about you. I can assure you, though, that the idea of family will show up on a Sunday morning very soon."

He gets up and walks around the room and sits back down.

"Actually, if you hadn't called me I was planning to call you. There's something we need to talk about."

"Did something happen to Hannah?"

He shakes his head. "No, as far as I know she's fine."

"Momma?"

Mark shakes his head. "I haven't heard from your mother since that call you already know about, but this does concern her, and indirectly you as well."

I'm getting nervous, and Frankie can tell. She gets up from where she was laying and comes over to sit beside me.

It's not like Mark to have trouble talking, but it's like he can't get started. Finally he says, "I got a phone call from Mrs. Alder yesterday."

I don't know who that is, so I shrug my shoulders. "What does that have to do with Momma and me?"

Then it hits me, about the time Mark says, "She was here when you first came around, only spoke to you once, and soon after that moved to be closer to her family.

"She is still sharp mentally, even at her age, and remembers you well. She said you reminded her of a relative named Natalie, a first cousin once removed."

I nod. "I remember now. She was standing off by herself and kept looking at me."

Mark looks through some papers on his desk. "She told me what she could remember about Natalie. Evidently she lost contact with her not long after she got married." He finds what he's looking for and reads out loud. "She got married in a hurry, I remember that. She must have been head over heels for this man Nathaniel." Mark stops and looks up at me.

I don't say anything right at first. I sit back in the chair and stare at the ceiling for a minute and then look back at Mark. "Sure sounds like Momma is her cousin."

"I believe so," says Mark. "And that is why I wanted to talk to you. I have to admit I'm in a bit of a dilemma here. She wants to talk to you, Boone, and I'm sure she would want to talk to your mother as well."

"Yeah."

"It's not that I want to keep your birth family from reuniting," he says. "My question is, how to proceed. I'm fairly certain that Mrs. Alder and your mother are related, but I'm not completely sure. I would hate to tell either one of them about the other without knowing, especially given Mrs. Alder's age and your mother's situation."

I sit there for a minute and then start laughing. Mark looks at me like I'm crazy or something, and when I can stop laughing I say, "You know, when that happened with Molly and Sylvia last night, the first thing I thought of was to come see you. Now I'm sitting here and you lay all this on me and the first thing in my head is I need to talk to Molly."

Mark nods. "She's family."

"So, are you asking me what to do about this? I got to say I don't have the first damn clue."

"I told Mrs. Alder I'd get back to her in a day or two," says Mark. "By all means talk this over with Molly. She is, as I may have mentioned before, an extraordinary young woman."

"You got that right," I say.

"And then there's Hannah," Mark says. "She's part of the family too."

Tell the truth, I hadn't even thought about Hannah until just now. She finally got out from under Aunt Claire and is doing good with the Coopertons. I sure don't want to do anything to screw that up. Momma is already talking about trying to get her back, whatever that means. I'm pretty sure Momma's not in any kind of place to take care of a teenage girl, but I bet as soon as she thinks she has any chance she'll try. Hannah doesn't even know she's got a . . . .

"Hey, Mark, what is Mrs. Alder? Is she my aunt,

or my great aunt, or what?"

"I was curious about that, so I found a chart on the internet and if I'm reading it right, if your mother is her first cousin once removed, you are her first cousin twice removed."

All this doesn't make one damn bit of sense to me. If I ever meet Mrs. Alder, I'm sure as hell not going to call her my cousin. She's way too old. And that removed stuff is, well, I don't know what it is.

"Okay, Mark, I guess I don't really care about all that stuff. What are we going to do next?"

Mark says, "I'm going to think about it, and pray about it, and you're going to talk to Molly about it. How much work do you have lined up?"

"The guy I'm on right now and two more after that. This job is maybe two more days, and I haven't told the other two when I'm going to start, so I can do whatever."

"Good," he says. "Call me in a day or two."

I sit in my truck in the parking lot and call Molly. Frankie is curled up on the passenger side, waiting for us to get going. When she answers I say, "I'm down at Mark's, and I need to talk to you. Okay if I come over tonight? It'll be kind of late when I get there."

"Sure, sweetie. What's wrong?"

"I think I'd better tell you when I get there. It's a hell of a mess."

Chapter Three

After I finish laying it all out for Molly she shakes her head. "You weren't kidding, sweetie. It's a hell of a mess."

I nod. "Right."

"So what are you going to do? I mean, you can't just keep them apart, can you? If you know Mrs. Alder's looking for her relatives, you kind of have to tell her."

Sylvia has been listening but hasn't said anything so far. She leans forward now and says, "I know it may not be my place to say anything, but if she's around my age, I can tell you that connecting with family is really important."

I look over at her. I don't think I've ever seen her this uncomfortable. It makes me wonder what Molly said to her about us.

"Sylvia, as far as I'm concerned, you and Molly are family to me, a hell of a lot more than this Mrs. Alder. You can say whatever you want to."

She gets up and almost runs out of the room, dabbing at her eyes. Molly looks over at me.

"Sweetie, sometimes you know exactly the right thing to say." She turns her chair. "I'll be right back. I need to check on Gram."

Frankie and I are waiting for them to get back, and I start thinking about Momma. It kind of scares me that I can hardly remember what she was like before my brother Frankie died. That just all but killed her, and if she had any fight in her before that she sure didn't after. Daddy ran all over her, treated her like shit, and she took it. Then, when she finally got herself out from under him, I'll be damned if she didn't pick up with somebody just about like him.

To hear her tell it, she's out on her own now and doing fine, but I don't know. That's a lot of years of one kind of life to just turn your back on, and start a whole different life. I don't know if I believe she's really turned everything around. It's taken me years to let go of most of that shit Daddy taught me, and I know he's still in there somewhere. That scares me sometimes.

Mark says that if Momma wants Hannah back, the state will probably let that happen unless she's in really bad shape. I can't see how that's a good idea, since she's just now figuring out how to stand up on her own, but I don't reckon they'll ask me what I think about it.

I keep expecting that the next time I hear from Momma she's going to be telling me about some new man she's started hanging out with. I hope to hell I'm wrong about that.

By the time Molly and Sylvia come back I'm feeling really bad, thinking about Momma and what a shitty life she's had so far.

"Are you okay, sweetie?" Molly rolls over and lays her hand on my arm.

I nod and say, "Just thinking about Hannah and Momma and what in the hell I'm going to do about all this."

"I was wondering," says Sylvia. "Does it have to be you? I mean, is it your responsibility?"

"She wants to see me," I say. "If she asks about Momma I got to have something to tell her."

"Just tell her where your mother is now and let her decide what to do next." Molly is still right there beside me. "It's really not your job to get them together."

I look at them, the two of them trying so hard to help me figure out what to do, and I think about what Mark said, that this is what families do, and I can't remember one single goddamn time that we ever did this with Momma and Daddy and me and Frankie and Hannah, and I can feel it coming on and I can't stop it. Then I'm crying, leaning over my knees with my head in my hands, and Molly is holding on to me on one side and Sylvia comes over on the other. Frankie scoots up next to my feet but she doesn't push them off me.

It takes me a minute to get myself back together, and finally I straighten up and say, "I'm sorry," and start to get up. Molly locks on to me with both arms and says, real soft, right in my ear, "You're not going anywhere right now, sweetie. You're staying right here with me. Okay?"

I stay for about another half hour or so. We talk about everything except Momma and Mrs. Alder, and Sylvia opens a bottle of wine.

"Not as fancy as what Raymond gave you, I'm sure," she says, "but it'll do, I think."

After one glass I stand up. "I need to get on home. Tomorrow and the next day I'll be at this new job, and that old barn is full of all kinds of stuff. I probably need to hit it pretty early, try to wrap it up by the end of the week."

Molly says, "I was going to tell you you could stay here with me, or I could go home with you, but I guess you're right. You'd better go. Call me tomorrow, or just come by after you finish."

"If I don't need to go back to see Mark again I'll just come on over when I get done."

I turn to Sylvia. "Thanks, Sylvia. Sorry to bust in on you so late."

She comes over to me and gives me a hug, one

that goes on for a while, and I'm thinking, we never did this in my old family either. She lets go and steps back. "You come by here anytime, Boone, anytime at all."

Molly goes with me as far as the door. "Nothing like a crisis to take your mind off of things, right?"

I'd forgotten all about what happened last night. At the time I thought it was a really big deal, but now I can't remember why I got so bent out of shape.

I squat down and say, "Girl, you are the best thing that's ever happened to me, you know that?"

"Of course I know that," she says. "And it's woman, remember?"

The barn this guy wants cleared out is about half the size of the one at our old house, but it's jam packed with all kinds of stuff. There's no room to walk into the place, so I start at the door and by the time I get halfway into the main part of the barn I've got a load.

He must have been watching, because when I pull up to the house he's opening the back door. He takes a quick walk around the truck and says, "All this can go." I'm hoping that's how it'll be every time. Otherwise this could take a lot longer than I planned for.

Frankie stays in the truck at the dump while I unload the back. The stuff I'm unloading looks like it's been in the barn for twenty or thirty years, so I don't even think about keeping any of it. It's almost all furniture, and wasn't much good when it was new.

I'm about to finish getting the second load out of the barn when I come across a chest of drawers that's damn near too heavy for me to move. I take the drawers out and carry them outside separately so I can get the chest outside and into the truck. I figure I'll put it back together in the truck bed and make that the last thing for this load.

When I get up to the house he takes one look at the chest of drawers and says, "So that's where it's been! I moved in here when my brother got a job out on the West Coast, and that matches what's in the bedroom." He takes a closer look. "Man, that thing is filthy. If you'd take that to your place and clean it up I'd give you an extra day's pay. I really hate cleaning."

"You want the clothes and stuff that's in it?"

He shakes his head. "Nah. If there's any books or papers or anything like that, I'll want those, but anything else can go to the dump."

So I get an extra day's pay for a couple of hours work, and a bag full of stuff for Goodwill. There's a locked metal box that feels kind of heavy, but I don't try to open it.

The next morning I unload the chest of drawers and give him the box. He weighs it in his hand, gives it a shake, and says, "I'll give Brad a call this evening and ask him where the key is. You want to help me get it in the bedroom?"

It takes a little while to get it in the house, but I still get the rest of the barn cleaned out by the end of the day. He doesn't want anything else off the truck, so I'm good to go. When he comes down to have a last look at the barn he says, "I guess I'm going to need you to clear out all around this. It's not such a bad building now that it's empty."

I tell him I can't do it right away, since I've got two people already on my list, but I can call him when I'm close to finishing the second one.

It wasn't much of a job, but the good part about it was it helped me not think about Momma and Mrs. Alder and Hannah, at least for a while.

I'm supposed to be at Mark's office as soon as I can after I get finished for the day. I'm pulling into the parking lot just about the time everybody's leaving, and Frankie and I stay in the truck until Betty is in her car and gone. I don't feel like answering any questions, and ever since things between me and Nancy fell apart, it's been hard to talk to Betty.

Mark is waiting for me, and I'm not even in my chair before he says, "I heard from Mrs. Alder again. She's insistent on seeing you, as soon as she can. She doesn't drive, and is doing all this without her family's knowledge. She wants you to come to her."

"Where is she?" He's not even letting me catch my breath here, but Mark doesn't get worked up about much of anything, and something's really got him going.

"Outside of Murfreesboro, in Middle Tennessee. A couple of hours from here, more or less."

"Okay, so what's the big hurry?"

Mark looks at me and I say, "Come on, man, me and you have been through some stuff together. I can tell when you're all cranked up about something. I figure if it's about this I ought to know what it is."

"Okay," Mark says. "She didn't want me to tell you this, but you're right, you need to know what's going on. Her health problems are getting worse, so even though her mind is sharp, she's feeling a sense of urgency about settling matters."

"What kind of health problems are you talking about?"

"If she wants you to know the details, she can tell you. I'll leave that up to her."

I sit back in the chair. This is all coming at me so fast I can't hardly keep it straight.

"All right, let's say that we can go see her. There's some stuff I need to figure out before that. Do we tell Momma, or Hannah, or Mrs. Cooperton about Mrs. Alder?"

Mark leans back in his chair and stares at the ceiling. He's still looking straight up when he says, "I would say no, and here's why. Mrs. Alder is still very capable mentally, and if she asks about your family, my gut tells me you should just lay it all out and let her decide what to do."

I grin. "That's pretty much exactly what Molly said I should do."

He waggles his finger at me. "I told you she was sharp. Don't you dare let that girl go, Boone."

"Woman. She calls me on it every time I call her a girl. Since she's not here, I guess it's up to me."

Now Mark's grinning, too. "I stand corrected."

Chapter Four

Molly and I have our first big fight about the trip to see Mrs. Alder. I want her to go with me and Frankie, and she wants to send me and Frankie off by ourselves.

"Dammit, Molly, I can't do this without you," I say. I'm looking down at the floor, mainly because I don't want to let her see how mad I'm getting.

"Sweetie, I can't go right now. Gram needs me."

"Bullshit. She can do without you for a day or two. She did fine for the two weeks we were in Virginia."

"You're not being fair," she says, and her voice is getting louder. "You're trying to get me to choose between you and Gram. Can't you just understand that I can't leave her right now?"

I don't see what the big deal is about her being gone for one night, two at the most, and I tell her so. The way Frankie is acting I can tell my voice is getting louder, too, and Frankie can tell I'm getting real mad. She's not sure what to do, but she's sticking right with me, up tight against the chair I'm sitting in.

"Look," she says. "It's not like you're in trouble or anything. You're just going to tell her how to get in touch with your mom and let her do whatever with that."

"So you think I'm just going to waltz in there and say hi, here's Momma's phone number, I think she's maybe living somewhere around Chicago, but I don't know for sure, and get back in the truck and drive off?"

"How the hell should I know what you're going to do?" I look up at her and she's so mad she's shaking, and her hands are white from gripping the chair arms so hard. I don't know why that pisses me off even more, but it does.

I start to say something, but she's not done.

"And don't you dare say bullshit when I tell you that Gram needs me. You have no idea what she's done for me. She practically saved my life, and if she says she needs me, or even if she doesn't say so and I know she does, then I'm going to do whatever I need to do."

"All right, then, what's so damn important?"

"Like I'm going to tell you!"

I stand up. "Fine. Come on, Frankie, let's get out of here."

I get home and damn near slam the door on

Frankie's tail. She heads for the bedroom and I walk around, fighting with myself to keep from picking something up and bouncing it off the wall.

I keep running it over in my head and it always comes out the same way. I'm going to get there and, when she finds out that I'm her second cousin twice removed or whatever the hell it was that Mark said I am, she's going to ask about what it was like being Momma's kid. Hell, she'll probably ask about Daddy, too.

I think about what it was like in that house and it makes me sick to my stomach. I don't even like to think about that any more, and I sure don't want anybody asking me questions about it. It won't do any good for her to find out what an awful life Momma lived, or what happened to my brother, or that we never went on trips or had any presents on Christmas, or that Daddy used to hit Momma whenever he was drunk enough and mad enough, which was a lot. I'm afraid I might slip up and tell her what really happened to Daddy. The more I think about this the worse it seems like it's going to be. I'm supposed to go over to the place she's staying day after tomorrow, and I'm already dreading it and wondering if there's any way out of going.

This job I'm on right now is real easy, and I'm getting a lot of this kind of thing. An old woman, lives by herself in a house she's been in for years, decides to get rid of a bunch of stuff because she's moving to one of those assisted living places, or to a place in Florida that already has furniture and not much room for her stuff, or in with her kids, or she's tired of seeing stuff that reminds her of how things used to be every time she turns around. The one I'm on right now isn't the main house. It's a little building out back next to the garden and she and her husband both used it for a bunch of different things. There's garden tools, easels and stuff for painting, and a bench with a whole bunch of tools I don't see how anybody could use until the old lady tells me her husband used to do scale models of all kinds of things, mostly war stuff, which doesn't make any sense to me but I guess you need tools to work on really small things.

I swear, the stuff people throw away. If I took home everything that was still working or just needed a little cleaning I'd have to have a bigger place. A lot of it's in good enough shape that I could open a store.

When I think about that the first thing I think of is that I could get the stuff in some kind of shape and Molly could run it, and that stops me right there.

I figure she must be really pissed since she hasn't called me since I left her house night before last. Course I haven't called her either. After the time we spent together over the winter and that trip to see

Raymond and Charlotte, not having her around doesn't seem right.

"You know what Mark would say about that," I tell Frankie on the way to the dump for the last load of the day. She doesn't answer, as usual, but it's not like she needs to. I know damn well what he'd say.

The next day is a short one. I finish up early afternoon, and she pays me and gives me an extra ten bucks.

"Sylvia said you were a real hard worker," she says. "I guess you'll be doing this for her pretty soon, won't you?"

I don't say anything right away, and she says, "You know, when she moves into The Commons, up there in the Tri-Cities. Of course that won't be for at least a year, with their waiting list. That's an awful big house she's in right now. I'll bet there's a lot of memories in that place." She turns to go back inside. "I'm going to tell all my friends about you, Boone. You're a fine young man. Sylvia's granddaughter is such a treasure, and Sylvia talks about how glad she is that the two of you ended up finding each other. One less thing for her to worry about. Of course, if Molly really wants to stay in that big old house, that's a different story all together."

She closes the door, still talking but mostly to herself now and I stand there staring at the ground, calling myself every kind of fool I can think of, and finally Frankie makes a little noise and I snap out of it enough to get in the truck and head for home.

Tomorrow morning I'm supposed to meet Mrs. Alder at 11:30, and Mark said I should allow three hours but that I would gain an hour heading west. I'll take off about nine and if I get there early I'll find a place to take Frankie for a walk.

That is, if I can get my shit together enough to go. All I can think about right now is Molly and Sylvia, and try to figure out if I missed something that would have kept me from making such a damn fool out of myself.

"They should have told me," I tell Frankie. "You don't keep that kind of shit secret from family." But as soon as I say that I know it's not true. There were all kinds of secrets in my family, in Nancy's family, I'll bet in Tiny's family too. Plus as far as Molly and Sylvia are concerned, I'm not exactly blood, even if I'm as close to Molly as I've ever been to anybody in my life.

I go back and forth about a thousand times trying to decide whether or not to call her and by the time I decide to, it's too late. I tell myself I'll do it in the morning before I leave.

Nobody picks up when I call about 8:30, and I fumble around for a second and finally say, "Listen, Molly, I'm heading for Middle Tennessee in a few minutes. I'll call you when I get back. I'm real sorry for being such an asshole." I hang up and think about what a stupid message that was to leave while I'm getting in the truck and heading out. I'm really bad at that kind of thing, and it's worse when I feel as rotten as I do right now.

I end up taking the interstate almost all the way there and make it about a half hour early. The place she's staying is bigger that the one I used to work at, and I think about just parking there and walking the grounds with Frankie, but I know that if anybody did that at Betty's place she wouldn't like it at all, so I find a little picnic area off the road and walk Frankie around under the trees, killing the last half hour and getting myself all worked up worrying about what might happen when I meet with her.

The guy at the front desk stands up and comes around from behind it as soon as he sees me and Frankie come in the door.

"You can't bring a dog in here," he says.

This is already feeling like a real bad idea.

"I'm supposed to see Mrs. Alder at 11:30," I say, and he leans back over his desk to look at the book sitting there. I can tell from here it's one of those appointment books.

"You're not on the list," he says, "and you need to get that dog out of here."

I'm about to say the hell with it and go on back home when another guy comes out of an office right behind the front desk.

"Everything okay here, Samuel?"

The first guy, Samuel, points at Frankie and says, "This kid doesn't have an appointment and he's trying to bring a dog in here. We don't allow dogs off the street to come in here."

I start to tell him I'm not a kid when the office guy says, "Why don't we go out front and talk for a moment?"

He doesn't wait for me to say anything, just goes past me and heads for the door.

I take another look at Samuel before I turn. He's already heading back to his chair and isn't paying any attention to me at all.

The office guy is waiting for me. He sticks out his hand. "Mr. Inglewood. And you are?"

I shake his hand. "Boone. and this is Frankie."

He looks down at Frankie. "A beautiful animal. It's Samuel's job to make sure people who come through that door have business here. You understand."

I nod.

He waits for a second and then says, "So do you have business here, Mr. Boone?"

"Boone is my first name," I say, "and Mrs. Alder wanted to see me. She was at the place I used to work before she came here."

"Oh?" he says. "And where was that?"

I tell him and he says, "Well, well. How is Betty doing these days? I haven't spoken to her in a month or more."

I guess he likes Betty, because he's a lot nicer to me and Frankie after I tell him about working there.

"Do they still have that black chaplain?" The way he says it makes me think he doesn't like Mark very much.

"Mark? He's still there," I say. I don't want to get in the middle of anything here. I can't tell if he doesn't like black people, or just Mark, or if I'm making all this up. "Me and him got along real well."

He gives me a look. "I see," is all he says, but it sounds like he doesn't think much of Mark.

"So can I see Mrs. Alder? She remembered me from when she was at Betty's place, and I guess I remind her of somebody she's kin to."

"I'll check," he says, "but I'm afraid Samuel was right about your dog."

I shrug. "Mostly Frankie was outside when we worked at the home anyway. If you could tell Mrs. Alder we're here, we can wait outside. Do y'all have a courtyard like Betty's place does?"

He nods and starts walking. "I'll show you where you can wait and I'll check with Mrs. Alder."

Frankie and I spend the next fifteen minutes wandering around. The courtyard looks a lot like Betty's, except bigger, and it looks like it connects to another one just like it in the middle of another bunch of buildings. Definitely bigger than Betty's place.

"Boone? Would you come over here please?"

I look around and there's Mr. Inglewood, and Mrs. Alder is walking beside him. She looks about the same as the last time I saw her, and when she sees me looking at her she smiles and waves.

Frankie and I head that way, and we meet out in the middle of the courtyard. There's a bunch of benches all around, and Mr. Inglewood helps Mrs. Alder to one and turns to me.

He talks real quiet, like he doesn't want her to hear him. "She's very happy you came, but I must tell you she tires very easily. I'll come back around in about fifteen minutes and see how you two are doing."

He steps back and turns to her. "Frances, I'll be back in a bit to look in on you, okay?"

She nods, and he walks back to the door they came out of.

She looks up at me. "He told you I tire easily, right?"

I nod.

She shakes her head. "Arthur is a wonderful administrator, but he has his fussy side." She pats the bench next to her. "Please sit down, Boone. I'm so very glad you came."

Chapter Five

I'm sitting in Mr. Inglewood's office, and Frankie is right next to me. He's sitting behind a big desk, and Samuel is leaning against the door.

He looks at me. "I'm trying to decide whether to ask you to leave or have Samuel throw you out. I come back after fifteen minutes and she's just sitting there weeping. What did you say to her?"

I figure most of this isn't any of his damn business, but I remember that it's going to be his job to take care of her after I'm gone. So I tell him, "She figured out that my mother was one of her relatives, first cousin once removed or something like that. So she wanted to know how Momma was doing, and I told her."

He doesn't say anything, just sits there.

After a minute I say, "She had a really rough life with Daddy, before she finally had all she could take and took off. He's gone, I figure for good, and Momma's somewhere up in Illinois at one of those women's shelters, trying to get her act back together."

He shakes his head at me. "You foolish child."

I stand up and so does Frankie. Samuel looks like he's about ready to do something, but I don't make any kind of move. I just say, "First of all, I'm not a child. Second, I didn't even tell her the really bad stuff. So you'd best just back off." There's a couple more things I want to say, but I don't.

He doesn't say anything.

Then he leans back in his chair, and things get a little less tense. He looks at the ceiling for a minute and then back at me. "All right, let's start over. And my apologies for calling you a child. That was unprofessional. Tell me about what was going on when I arrived."

"She was just having a good cry, man. I've done that myself thinking about the lousy deal Momma had. I don't know why you're all bent out of shape about this."

He nods. "How did you leave things with her?"

"She wanted to know how to get in touch with Momma and Hannah, that's my sister. She has Mark's number already, and he told me before I came down here that he'd let Momma and Hannah know about her and put them all in touch with each other."

Inglewood shakes his head. "He always did like sticking his nose in where it didn't belong. Guess some things never change." I can feel my face getting red, and I shift around in my chair.

Then I'm back on my feet again, and this time so is Inglewood. We're looking at each other across that big desk, and Frankie is growling a little, so low I don't think anybody but me can hear her.

I'm so mad I can barely get the words out, but I try to keep my voice under control.

"Now, I don't know what's going on between you and Mark, and I don't want to know. It's none of my damn business, but I'll tell you this. That guy you're bad mouthing probably saved my life, and he's taught me more about being a man than my daddy ever did. So you might want to be careful what you say about him."

We're staring at each other and I'm not sure what's going to happen next when Samuel says, "Uh, sir?"

We both turn at the same time. Mrs. Alder is in the doorway. She walks straight up to me and puts her hands on my shoulders.

"I'm sorry about the little crying spell, Boone, and I'm glad I caught you before you had to leave. You have no idea how much it means to me, knowing that Natalie is free from that awful man and working on putting her life in order."

"Ma'am, you don't need to apologize for crying. I was just telling him," I point at Inglewood, "that I've done the same thing a time or two, thinking about what all Momma's been through. I've even heard tell it's good for you every now and then."

That gets a little laugh, and she pats me on the cheek. "I'm kind of tired after all that, and I think I will go lie down for a bit. You come back and see me, Boone. You are welcome to visit me anytime." She nods. "Anytime."

I look over at Inglewood.

She catches the look and I guess she knows what it means, because she says, "Isn't that right, Arthur?"

He nods once. "Of course, Frances. If you will vouch for him, we will be glad to put him on the approved list."

I'm looking at him and trying hard not to smile. I bet that was really hard for him to say.

"I'll definitely do that, ma'am," I say. "Come on, Frankie, we've got a drive in front of us."

"Damn, I wish Molly had been with us," I tell Frankie when we're back out on I-40 heading home. She could have dealt with Samuel and Inglewood, and I sure would have liked her to be there when Mrs. Alder started crying. I really had no idea what to do about that, and I bet Molly would have known.

I get home in plenty of time to call Mark, and I start to tell him what happened and then say, "I think it'd be better if I came down there. I don't start my next job for a couple of days."

He tells me to come on right now unless I'm too tired of driving, and I tell him I'm heading for the truck as soon as I hang up. I need to talk to him about a bunch of stuff, and I'd rather do it now than put it off.

He meets me in the parking lot and says, "You had anything to eat yet?" When I say no he says, "You remember that deli we went to once when you still lived here? You and Frankie can follow me, and we'll sit outside where we can talk."

When I tell him I'd rather talk here at his office he doesn't answer for a minute, just studies me. Then he says, "I'm going to call them and put in our order, run over and pick up the sandwiches, and we can eat here. Come on inside and you two can wait in my office."

I spend the time he's gone trying to figure out what all I want to say. I got to tell him about me and Molly and what an asshole I was, and what I found out from the old lady I was working for, and how my talk with Mrs. Alder went, and find out what the hell is the deal with him and Inglewood.

By the time he gets back I've sort of got it figured out, but as soon as I smell the sandwiches I realize how hungry I am. I fed Frankie as soon as we got home, so she's okay, but it turns out I'm starving, and I don't say hardly anything until the food is all gone.

Mark is a lot slower than me but he finally gets

through most of his sandwich and pushes the rest of it off to one side. "Okay, Boone. Let's have it."

"I tell you, man, this is a big damn mess," I say. "While you were gone I was trying to figure out how to tell you, and I think I'm just going to lay it all out there."

I tell him about my fight with Molly, and about what the old lady said, and about Mrs. Alder. When I tell him about Inglewood, he holds up his hand and says, "Okay, tell me that part again."

After I run out of stuff to say we sit there for a minute and then he says, "First thing is, you need to make things right with Molly. What you two have is the real thing, anybody who sees you together can tell that. So that's number one."

He stops for a minute and goes on. "Let Molly tell you about Sylvia's upcoming move, if you can. I think it would be better coming from her than if you say you heard from somebody else."

He gets up and comes around the desk. "You want some coffee? I'm going down to the cafeteria,"

I tell him no and in a minute he's back with two cups. "In case you change your mind."

He sips and sets the cup down. "Now, about me and Arthur. This goes way back, Boone, and there are some details I won't share with you. I can tell you that he and I were in school together and there was an, an incident involving Arthur that I was aware of, and, when I was asked about it, I told them what I knew."

I sit back and reach for the cup of coffee without thinking about it. I take a couple of sips, set it down, and say, "That's what he meant by you sticking your nose into other people's stuff."

Mark nods.

"Well, I don't know what the hell to do about that."

"I would say the best thing to do is nothing. It's not anything you would even know about except for this conversation, and doesn't have anything to do with your relationship with Mrs. Alder."

I shrug. "I'd be okay with not having to deal with him at all. He acted like he was better than me from the minute I met him, and people like that just piss me off. So whatever bad blood you two have between you, I'm fine with leaving it alone.

"So, what are we going to do about Hannah and Momma? And I was thinking on the drive back, is Aunt Claire going to get in the middle of this? I'm telling you, man, it's wearing me out just thinking about it."

Mark laughs out loud. "Yes, I can understand that. I would like to talk to Mrs. Alder again before I take any kind of action. If she wants me to prepare Hannah and your mother for the phone call, I'll be glad to. I can also just give her their numbers and let her take care of it herself."

"What about Mrs. Cooperton? Does she need to know that Hannah might be getting a phone call from Mrs. Alder?"

Mark nods. "I'm going to mention that to Mrs. Alder. She's been very good for Hannah and I don't think it would be right to surprise her with this kind of news.

"Your Aunt Claire is a real wild card in all of this. I'll ask Mrs. Alder about that as well. You got the impression she was in good shape mentally?"

I nod. "Better than almost everybody here at this place." I see the look on his face and say, "I didn't mean that like it sounded."

"I know, Boone."

We sit and sip coffee for a bit and he says, "I don't think we've spoken since your trip to see your friends in Virginia."

I tell him about Raymond and Charlotte, and I got to say it feels pretty good to talk about that after all the shit I laid on him about everything else.

"It was really good, Mark. Molly sure loved that library of theirs," and I stop talking and look down at the floor.

Mark looks at his watch. "It's not too late to call her and tell her you're back in town. You can call her from here if you like."

I shake my head. "I'll do it as soon as we get back

home. We better hit the road.   Thanks, man. I appreciate you."

He grins. "This might be the first serious conversation we've had where you didn't accuse me of getting too preachy."

"That's why I'm leaving. Don't want to give you a chance."

He laughs and stands up. "Let me know how it goes with Molly."

Chapter Six

How it goes with Molly is kind of weird.

She doesn't ask me about the meeting with Mrs. Alder, or about the drive, or anything, It's like she doesn't want to know about it.

It kind of freaks me out because she was real interested in me connecting with some of my family, even though it's a part I didn't even know I had until I was working at the home and met Mrs. Alder. Now when I bring it up she finds something else to talk about, and about half the time it feels like she's bringing stuff up she doesn't really care anything about.

She wants to know how my last job went, and that's hard, too, because that old woman is the one who told me that Sylvia was looking to move to an assisted living place. Mark said I shouldn't let on like I know until Molly brings it up, and I think that's a good idea, but it's awful damn hard to not say anything.

A couple of times I catch Molly looking at me kind of funny, like she knows something's going on but she can't quite figure out what it is. I try to pretend that nothing's going on but it's hard.

The jobs are still coming in pretty steady, and I'm glad about that, mainly because it gives me something else to talk to Molly and Sylvia about. They're all new customers right now, but they are all pretty close by, and I'm not real interested in driving a long ways. I'm still hauling perfectly good stuff to the dump, but not always. The one I'm on right now is different.

First off, it's a young guy. Not as young as me, but I'm used to dealing with old people and he looks like he could do the stuff he's talking about asking me to do for him. Plus, he's not throwing anything away, and he told me he can explain it better in person than on the phone.

I pull up into his driveway and, back behind the house, there's a brand new metal building that is twice as big as most of the barns around here. He meets me in the driveway, sticks out his hand, and says, "Corey Stinnett. You're Boone, right?" I nod. "Come on back here and take a look at this."

He stops when he sees Frankie. "Not sure if I can let that dog in here. I can't have him chewing on anything or lifting his leg anywhere."

"Frankie's a she, and she won't do any of that," I

say. "If I tell her to leave stuff alone, she will."

"Okay," he says, but he sounds like he might not believe it. "You'd better be right about that."

There's a regular size door off to the side of one of those big garage doors, and when we get inside it's almost pitch black. He reaches over to a bunch of switches and hits them all, and the place lights up from one end to the other.

It's about half empty and he's got it divided up with some walls that just come up around chest high. The floor is concrete, and he's got big wide walkways down the middle and over close to both side walls.

He starts walking down the middle of the building. "You know John Rice Irwin?"

I shake my head and realize he can't see me since he's about five steps ahead. "No, can't say that I do."

"He was a collector of all kinds of things and ended up creating the Museum of Appalachia because he outgrew his house and his barn and every other place on his property. If you've never seen it you ought to sometime. It's pretty impressive."

I don't say anything. I've never been to a museum of any kind, and don't know that I'm going to start now.

"Well, what I'm doing here is going to be more discriminating than Mr. Irwin. From the look of things, he hauled home everything he ran across. I plan to be a lot pickier than that. And this," he waves his arm around, "is my storage building. I do love this area, and I want to celebrate it, but not by saving everything. People are doing that already.

"What I need is somebody who can help me with cleaning, organizing, and storing what I collect."

I don't say anything.

He looks back over his shoulder. "What do you think?"

I'm not sure what to say to the guy, so I look around like I'm interested.

"It wouldn't be steady work, you understand," he says.

"What does that mean, exactly?"

"If you work out, I'll need somebody once or twice a month for about three days, give or take."

I try not to show it, but I'm thinking, this is just about perfect.

"You talking year-round?"

He nods. "Maybe not quite as often in January and February, but, yeah, pretty much year round."

He's walking again. We're about halfway down the middle aisle, and the sections we pass are mostly empty. Once in a while there'll be a box or a piece of furniture, and one place has a car.

He stops at the car.

"This is here because it was my grandfather's car. He bought it new, and it's got family sentiment connected to it. Most of the stuff I'm collecting is more of a representation of the region at a particular time."

He goes on like that for a while, and I don't really care one way or the other. I try to stay interested because it sounds like it might be a good job for me.

"So I might need you to meet me here to do the unloading, cleanup, and so on, or I might need you to help me pick up something I've found and can't fit in my car."

I look around. We're at the back of the building now, and I say, "Man, this is a big place," mainly because I can't think of anything else to say. This guy is like the opposite of all these other people I've been working for, wanting to get rid of stuff. He wants to get more stuff.

"You know, you have a good reputation," Corey says. "People say you show up when you say you're going to and work hard." He looks me up and down. "So, should we try this once, see if we can stand each other?"

I nod. We talk about money and he's going to pay me the same as the last few jobs I've had, so that's okay, and he says we can talk about whether or not to make it a long term thing after the first job. That's okay with me, too. I don't know how tied down I want to get. I kind of like doing a job I know is going to end in a couple of days.

The first job goes pretty well. It's all the two of us

can do to get the old pot-bellied stove into the back of my truck, and getting it out is even worse. Cleaning it takes forever, and I'm understanding now why he wanted to hire some help.

It cleans up real nice, though, and he's happy as a pig in shit. "Look at that beauty," he says to me when we've got it into one of the empty sections in his building. "This stove was in a general store on the Little Tennessee River for over fifty years. What I wouldn't give to hear some of the lies that were told around this thing."

It doesn't look all that special to me, but I'm glad Corey is happy. He pays me, adds an extra twenty, and says, "I've got my eye on a couple of things. I'll give you a call in a week or so."

"You know, Frankie," I tell her on the way home, "if I get a call from him every other week or so I might just need two or three more jobs a month."

Mark calls me a few days later. My next job doesn't start for two more days, and me and Frankie are mostly just hanging out.

"I talked to Mrs. Alder," he says. "She thinks it might be a good idea to wait to contact your mother until she calls you again and you can get a feel for how she's doing."

I don't say anything. What I'm thinking is, I do not want to be in the middle of this, but it looks like that's where I'm going to be like it or not.

I swear, it's like Mark's reading my mind. "She doesn't want you to be the middleman here, Boone. She wants to work things out with your mother herself, but I have to say I agree with her thoughts on this. Your mother is still working through the effect of a very rough past, and she will need to be in pretty good shape to be able to deal with something this big.

"If you can just let me know how she's doing the next time she calls, I'll take it from there. I'll call Mrs. Alder and help her figure out what to do next."

Besides Corey and his warehouse, I've got a couple of normal jobs, clearing brush for one old woman and cleaning out a shed for a guy who's getting ready to move to Florida. I can do this kind of thing in my sleep, so they don't help much in taking my mind off Momma and Hannah and Mrs. Alder. I'm about due to check in with Hannah again, and I know I can't tell her about all this. It's too much up in the air still. I make the call and we talk for a half hour or so and she sounds like she's doing great. After I hang up I think, what if this screws things up for her? Every time I think about this it gets more complicated.

If it wasn't for Molly being here, I'd be tempted to take off and settle somewhere else, not tell anybody where I ended up, and let everybody else sort all this shit out. I don't even think about asking her to cut and run with me, though. She wouldn't leave Sylvia even if things were going great, and I know they're not.

I guess now I'm just waiting for Momma to call.

Chapter Seven

I know Molly's still up when we get back to the house from one of Corey's projects, so I make sure Frankie has water and call her.

When she answers I say, "Hey, I wanted to let you know it was kind of a long day, but me and Frankie are home now."

There's a pause and she says, "Sweetie, there's some stuff we need to talk about."

Oh, man.

"Okay. When do you want to do that?"

I got a real bad feeling right now. She sounds awful serious. No, more like sad. Or scared.

"Not tonight. It's a little late, and this might take a while."

"Okay," I say again. This has been a really rough day already, and I'm about wrung out, so I can't think of anything else to say.

She's waiting for me to say something else, I guess, but finally gives up. "Can you come by and pick me up tomorrow? We can talk over at your place."

Most nights it takes me about half a minute to fall asleep, but I bet I don't get more than an hour all night long. I'm up earlier than usual, and it's hard to wait until I'm sure they're up before I call to let her know I'm on my way. She says that's fine, Sylvia is gone to the store and she'll leave her a note.

After I pick her up and bring her home, we sit in the living room for what seems like a real long time without either one of us saying a word. I'm about to ask her why she wanted to come over when she finally looks over at Frankie and, like she's talking to her, says, "So, is the work with Corey at that warehouse of his going okay?"

"Listen, can we talk about that some other time? I've been about half crazy ever since I talked to you last night and you sounded all serious like something bad was wrong. Is something bad wrong?"

She doesn't say anything, but her eyes fill up with tears and she starts crying and I don't know what I'm supposed to do.

I get up and go into the kitchen, mix a couple of S&Ss and hand her one when I get back. She says, "It's kind of early in the day, but what the hell," and takes a small sip. She sets it down and picks it right back up, takes another sip, and finally looks me right in the eyes.

"Gram is going to have to sell our house," she says, and that's all she can get out before she starts crying for real.

I take the glass out of her hand and put hers and mine both on the floor next to my chair. The only thing I know to do is wait for her to get a breath, and when she does I say, "How come?"

That was the wrong thing, I guess, because it starts her up again and it takes her a couple of minutes to settle back down. She points at her glass and I hand it to her.

"She's going to move into a place, a place called The Commons," she says, and I almost say, "I know," but I realize that would be really stupid so I catch myself.

"Is that, like, an apartment building?"

She shakes her head. "Gram's starting to forget things, get confused, stuff like that. It's a really nice place," and she's about to start again but catches herself, "and it's going to be a year or two before she can even get in there, but she, she doesn't have enough money to afford it without selling our house."

I know from working at Betty's place that when Sylvia moves in there Molly can't go with her. I bet that's what's really got her all upset.

Molly just talks, half to me and half to herself, for the next while, about how long Sylvia has been in that house, and what she remembers about when she was a little girl, going there for holidays and all that.

"Christmas is still a ways off," she says, "but I can't help thinking about it maybe being the last one we get to have there. You remember how nice it was last year, just hanging out?"

I nod. That was the only year I can remember having any kind of Christmas at all.

We sit without saying anything for a while and then Molly puts her hand on my arm. I've been waiting for her to let me know where this is going, and I think I'm about to find out.

Molly's looking at me now instead of at the floor or off into space. "What am I going to do, Boone?"

"You mean . . . ."

She nods. "When Gram sells the house and moves to The Commons."

I don't say anything right away, but I'm thinking, this is why she didn't want to go with me to see Mrs. Alder. She didn't want to go to the kind of place that Sylvia's headed to. I wonder if she'll ever go with me down to see Mark after this.

I look over at her and she's back to looking down at the floor.

"I've got plenty of room here." I say it before I think about it, and first she looks real glad and then she gets a look I know real well. I used to look like that a lot.

"I don't want your pity, Boone," she says, and it

sounds like me. Just like me.

I can't help it. I start laughing, and I think for a second she's going to throw her glass at me. I've never seen her this mad before.

"Wait a minute," I say.

"Just who the hell do you think you are?" She's shouting now. "How dare you!"

"Listen," I say. "Listen to me. You know when Mark was telling you about why he put me and Frankie in that picture, and he asked me if I thought the job at the home was a handout?"

She doesn't say anything.

"They offered me that job when I was about to get kicked out of Gamaliel's house. Even though I needed a place to stay, I almost told them to take that job and shove it up their ass, and you know why? I thought they were doing it because they felt sorry for me. I didn't want them to do something because they thought I was this poor kid they needed to help."

She nods.

"I don't pity you, Molly," I say. "And I wasn't laughing at you, I swear. That look on your face, right before you said you didn't want my pity, I was laughing because I know that look. That's my look."

She stares at me for a long minute.

"Show me."

"What do you mean?"

"You said it's your look. Show me," she says. She

leans back in the chair and folds her arms.

"Hell, I can't, I mean, just like that."

"Why not?"

I think about it. "Damned if I know. Okay, here it is."

I try to imagine somebody treating me like I'm some kind of charity case, and try to look at Molly like it's her doing it.

She doesn't react right away. Then her mouth twitches a little, and I can't help it. I start laughing again, and this time she does too.

"That," she says, shaking her head, "was just pitiful."

I shrug. "I know."

She asks about the warehouse job again and I figure she doesn't want to talk about Sylvia or about having to move any more. That's fine with me. My head is crammed so full of shit right now I can't even think straight. I feel like I ought to do something about some part of this mess, but I'll be damned if I know what that is.

Molly says, "You don't have anything to eat here, do you? I just realized I'm starving."

I get up and go to the kitchen and look in the fridge. It's about empty, like usual. There's half a pizza from sometime, maybe night before last, and some of that American cheese already sliced up and wrapped in plastic, and two bottles of beer and a bottle of Thunderstorm that's about half gone.

The counter isn't much better, but there is a bag of chips and I grab that. She looks at it when I bring it back and shakes her head.

"Let's go get something at that gas station, you know, the one that has the little deli inside. We can bring it back here and eat, and then I'd better get back to Gram's. She might be home already."

We're on our way back from the deli and Molly says, "You know, you can't talk about this with Gram until she brings it up."

I don't tell her, but that's exactly what Mark said about Sylvia's move to this Commons place when I found out about it from that lady three or four jobs ago. "Wait until Molly tells you," he had said, and it was all I could do to let her tell me. Now I've got it to do all over again.

Of course, I've been keeping secrets right along, so this is just one more. Daddy blowing his head off in the barn that morning, his grave in the back field, Gamaliel's money box, the whole moonshine thing. I did tell people about the moonshine, but I sure didn't say anything when they found the still up near where Jerry burned to death.

I've told a bunch of lies, I guess, when you think about it. The one about Daddy running off and leaving us has to be the biggest one, but I've told a lot. Still telling them, but none as big as that. Maybe that's why I have such a hard time hearing it when people tell me I'm a good worker, or a fine young man, or any of that other bullshit. I know better.

Maybe I ought to talk to Mark about this. I'm sure as hell not going to tell him about Daddy. I'm never telling anybody that one, but he knows about most everything else already. I'll give him a call, see when he's got some time.

Sylvia is home and fixing her afternoon cup of coffee with a drop of brandy.

"Can I make you two a cup?"

We both say yes, and when we're in the sunroom I'm about as uncomfortable as I was that time Sylvia was talking to me about doing the right thing by Molly. Now, it's like I'm on the outside of something; they keep looking at each other and then looking away, and finally Sylvia says, "You told him, didn't you?"

"Sorry, Gram, I just had to talk to somebody. It's all pretty overwhelming, you know?"

Molly is real red in the face and won't look at Sylvia, and she says, "It's all right, dear, we were going to have to tell him sooner or later."

The only thing I'm feeling right now is I'm glad I don't have to pretend I don't know this, especially since I've known for quite a while now. I start to tell them that and catch myself. Bad idea.

I look up and Sylvia is watching me. She sips her

coffee and sets the cup down.

"You know, Boone, you're the reason I'm doing this."

I don't know what the hell she's talking about, and from the look on Molly's face when I glance at her, she doesn't either.

Sylvia laughs. "You should see yourself, Boone. You look like you're caught in the headlights of a train headed straight for you."

I didn't see that one coming at all, and for a few seconds I just stare at her.

"Gram, what the hell are you talking about?" Molly had been kind of beside Sylvia, but now she swivels her chair around to face her. "How is this, this terrible thing, how is this Boone's fault?"

Sylvia shakes her head.

"Dear Molly, you have no idea how happy I am that Boone came along. I've known for quite some time that this decision was coming, but the thought of leaving you alone was terrifying.

"Seeing you two together has eased my mind tremendously. Boone's a good man, Molly. You hang on to him."

I can't believe this. I just had this conversation with Molly and it damn near wore me out, and here we are again. When I look over at Molly I can tell she's thinking the same thing.

"I never told you this," Sylvia is still talking, "but

you know my good friend Ruby?"

Molly nods.

"This has been, oh, four years ago, I think. Once when she and I were having an afternoon cup of coffee, she told me that the week before, she had been out shopping and gotten confused about where she was and how to get back home.

"She said, 'I had to call my nephew and get him to come get me. Thank goodness I remembered his number, or I might still be wandering around the mall.' She was laughing about it, passing it off as no big deal, but it made me think."

Sylvia stops for another sip of her coffee.

"You have grown into a fine, capable young woman, dear, but if that had been me out there at the mall instead of Ruby, I couldn't have called you to come get me."

I'm watching Molly, trying to figure out what she's thinking about all this. She's locked in on Sylvia, but cuts her eyes over to me every once in a while, not long enough for me to tell anything.

After what feels like a real long silence Molly says, "So you were just waiting for some man to come along to take care of me?" She sounds really pissed off, and then she and Sylvia both look over at me.

I figure I'd better say something, so I say, "Hell, Sylvia, I was kind of counting on her taking care of me."

I can see Molly's trying to stay mad, but when Sylvia starts laughing she can't keep it up, and she starts in laughing, too. They look at each other and then back at me, and Sylvia says, "Of course, Boone, that's what I had in mind all along."

Chapter Eight

I call Mark and tell him everybody knows everything about Sylvia and the house and all. I don't mention wanting to talk to him about all that other stuff. Maybe I'll just let that go for a while.

It's another two weeks before I hear from Momma. When she calls, she's calling from a real noisy place, and she's almost shouting into the phone.

I'm at Corey's warehouse, and we're trying to get his latest find cleaned up and ready to put in its place. He's got a pressure washer going, and it's pretty loud on my end, too, so I wave at him and point to the phone in my hand and then to the door. He nods, and I step inside the warehouse and pull the door shut.

"Momma, where are you? I can't hardly hear you."

"Wait just a minute," she shouts, and she must be moving because the sound's getting fainter. "Is this better?"

"Yeah, a lot. Where are you?"

"I got a job!" She sounds better than I've heard her in years, maybe ever. "You know that place I've been staying, that was helping me out when I finally got away from Jake, well, we share cooking there and when they tasted one of my pies, Rikki, she's in charge there, she said there was a bakery in town that was hiring and I should go talk to them."

"That's great, Momma," I say, and I really mean it. She sounds awfully good.

"So I'll be staying around here, at least for a while. I can't talk right now, my break's almost over, but I'll call you later. I gotta go," and she's gone.

When I call Mark to let him know about Momma, he says I ought to come down to see him. "You've got a fair amount of stuff going on right now, Boone. Why don't you and Frankie come down and we'll spend a little time together? And by all means bring Molly if you like."

"Face to face is probably a good idea. Give me until day after tomorrow and I'll be done with Corey's latest job and we can come down whenever works for you."

I'm not taking Molly along this time. I need to talk about me and her, and it wouldn't feel right to do that with her in the room. I might not be able to say what I need to say.

Mark looks disappointed when it's just me and Frankie that come through his door.

I don't wait for him to ask. "I have to talk to you about Molly, and I need it to be just you and me."

He frowns. "Is she okay?"

"She's fine. It's not that kind of thing."

After I lay it all out for him I say, "You know that time I was all freaked out by Sylvia pushing me to do the right thing? You told me that sometimes being in a family is hard, and I get that, but this . . . "

"This has a clock ticking," says Mark.

"Right."

"So even though she's never used the word, you believe that she expects you and Molly to get married, and sooner rather than later."

"Right."

He's quiet for a minute and then nods. "I think a part of what's going on here is that Molly sees herself as Sylvia's caretaker, and Sylvia sees herself as Molly's."

I don't say anything.

"It would be interesting to know if they've had a conversation about that, but in any case, your entry into the family has changed the dynamic. Changed it for the better, I would say." He's been staring at the ceiling, but now he drops his head and looks at me. "Now there are three voices in this conversation instead of two. Two voices going back and forth tend to get stuck, and maybe you can be the catalyst to change that."

I don't understand all that stuff about dynamics and voices, and I'm not even sure what a catalyst is or what I'm supposed to do if I am one. Sometimes I feel like he's mainly talking to himself and I just happen to be in the room. I start to say something about that when he shakes his head. "Let me think on that for a bit. Tell me about your phone call from your mother."

"Not much to tell," I say. "She sounded good, said she had a job and couldn't talk long because she was on break, and said she'd call soon."

I tell him about the rest of the call and he nods. "That is very good news, Boone. She's starting to stand on her own feet."

"Yeah, after she hung up I was trying to remember the last time I heard her sound like that and I couldn't."

Momma never stood on her own two feet, not the whole time I've been around. She was always either doing stuff for Daddy or us kids, or just sitting at that damn kitchen table staring off into space. It's a wonder she remembers how to be on her own.

"You know," Mark is saying, "you know what this means."

I shake my head.

"Maybe you don't have to worry so much about your mother, if she's doing this well."

I shrug. "Kind of soon to say. I mean, I thought

when she left Daddy she was doing good and then she took up with that son of a bitch Jake that ended up being an awful lot like Daddy."

Mark nods. "You're right, of course, although it sounds like she has a much better support system now than she had then. Plus, I would hope she has learned from her experience with Jake.

"I expect I'll hear from Mrs. Alder again before long. I may tell her that Natalie is sounding good and recommend that she give her some time being successful out on her own before getting in touch with her."

He grins at me. "So, other than your girlfriend, her mother, and your own mother, how are things? You have anything else going on I need to know about?"

"No, as far as I know, that's about it. This thing with Corey and his warehouse full of junk is going okay and maybe turning into a regular thing, but I'll be damned if I know what he's going to do with all that stuff."

"I wouldn't worry about that, unless he's doing something illegal. You don't want to get mixed up in anything else that would get you in trouble with the law."

I start to ask him what the hell he's talking about, but when I look at him he's looking at the bookshelf next to his desk. The jar of shine I left him is sitting right there.

"You ever going to drink that?" I say.

He shakes his head. "Probably not, Boone. I consider it a memento, and an empty jar wouldn't mean quite the same thing."

All I can think is, what a waste of the triple filtered stuff. Gamaliel would have told him just to drink the damn shine.

We talk a little longer, just about this and that, and I tell him about Molly wanting to go kayaking. She's heard about this guy down in Knoxville, Jim Brunton, that works on kayaks in his spare time and has a little group of people he goes out on the water with, and she wants to call him up and see if he can figure out some way to set things up so she can go out and paddle around.

"I assume you'll be going out with her," Mark says.

"I guess so," I say. "Never been out on a boat, unless you count that Mississippi River cruise with P.J. and Joaquin. This kayak thing sounds like a lot of work to me, but she wants to try it."

"You understand what a big deal this is for her," Mark says. "Remember how she lost the use of her legs? Going back into the water in any way is a huge step, even if it's on a calm lake in a boat instead of diving into a mountain stream."

I hadn't thought about that at all, but I can see

what he's talking about. "Well, she wants to get in touch with him next week, so we'll see what happens."

"I can't wait to hear about this," he grins.

This guy Jim says he wants to set one up so it's impossible to flip over, he calls it capsizing, so he says give him a week or two. It ends up taking him a little longer, but when Molly gets a call from him she calls me all excited.

"When can we go out on the lake? Jim works during the week, so he said it would have to be a weekend. Are you doing anything this next Sunday? He wants to go out on a lake instead of a river, so there's almost no current to worry about."

I got to say it's a lot more fun than I thought it would be. He has one that holds two people, so me and Molly go out together, and it has these things out on the side that keep it from tipping too much one way or the other. He has one of his own boats and goes out with us, and we just paddle around this little island and back to the shore.

My arms are already getting tired, and I think Molly's are too, but she has the biggest grin on her face and just keeps thanking Jim over and over.

I help him with getting the boats back on the roof of his van and when he's ready to pull out I say, "Listen, man, that was great. She had a really good time. What do I owe you?"

He shakes his head. "Are you kidding? This was as much fun for me as it was for you. I like solving problems, and this was a new one. You don't owe me a thing."

There's just a second of that old feeling of not wanting any kind of charity from anybody, but it doesn't last. I stick out my hand. "Thanks, man. It was great, except my arms are going to be sore tomorrow."

He laughs. "Oh, yeah. You don't realize all the muscles you're using until you've done it a few times. Molly might be better off than you. She's used to using her arms a lot."

Molly rolls up about that time and Jim says, "It won't be long until the weather gets kind of iffy about getting out on the water, but you two call any time you want to go back out and we'll see if we can make it happen."

The whole ride back Molly is talking about how much fun it was, and when we get back to Sylvia's, she's still telling her about it when I get Frankie in the truck and head home.

"Next time I'll ask about a kayak for you, girl," I say.

Chapter Nine

I'm between jobs and me, Molly, and Frankie are at the park doing a whole lot of nothing. We've got a lunch packed and a ball for Frankie to chase, the shady spot just off the paved walking trail we like best is empty when we get here, so we're set up for the afternoon. Molly has a pretty good arm and she's about got Frankie worn out, and I'm about half asleep when my phone rings.

"Hey, man," Tiny says. "You in the middle of something?"

"Hell, yes, I'm in the middle of something. Right about halfway between a lunch and a nap. I'm not working on any jobs right now so me and Molly and Frankie are working hard at not doing a damn thing."

He doesn't answer and I think maybe we got cut off, and then he says, "Okay, that's cool. Listen, I'll let you get back to it."

"Hold on, man," I say. He's sounding weird, like

something's bothering him. "I was just giving you shit. What do you need?"

"I don't want to bust in on your day off," he says, and I'm thinking I've never heard him this serious. "I'll talk to you some other time."

"Hey, Tiny," I say, but he's already gone.

Man, I don't want to have to think about this. Up until now the last few weeks have been pretty smooth. No more calls from Momma, but the last time I talked to Hannah she'd heard from her and got the same kind of feeling that I did, that Momma's doing pretty good. Mrs. Alder is letting Momma get her act together before she calls her, and I've been down one more time to see her. This time Molly came along, and, just like I thought, she took care of Inglewood and Samuel without even breaking a sweat. She and Mrs. Alder got along great, and we had to promise to come back and visit her again soon.

Guess Mark was right when he said I didn't have to get in the middle of all this stuff with my old family. It's working itself out just fine.

It's still a little weird with Sylvia, but me and Molly are okay. At least I think we are. We don't talk about Sylvia selling her house or moving or what might happen with Molly, but I guess sooner or later we're going to have to. I'm fine with putting that off as long as I can.

"You know what we ought to do, sweetie?" Molly is

out of her chair and on the blanket next to me, and Frankie is passed out a few feet away.

"What's that?"

"Next time we ought to bring Bert and Ray with us, and maybe Gram, too."

"Okay," I say, "but it'd take both of them to bring that ball back. We'd have to bring a smaller ball for them to chase."

"We could do that," she says. She lies back on the blanket and lays her hand on my stomach. We stare up through the leaves and I'm just about to nod off when she says, "What did Tiny want on the phone?"

I stretch my arms back over my head. "I don't know. Wouldn't tell me what's going on with him. He sounded really strange, too."

She might have said something else, but I'm not sure. Next thing I know it's an hour or so later and Frankie's poking me with her nose. Molly is sound asleep. I watch her for a minute or two and I guess she can tell, because she opens her eyes and says, "I thought somebody was staring at me. How long have you been awake?"

"Just a minute or two. Frankie woke me up. I think she's ready to go."

We've been back at my place for an hour or so when Tiny calls me again.

"Hey, Boone."

This doesn't sound like Tiny at all. No joking

around, no asking about Frankie or Molly.

"Are you okay, man? You sound really weird."

"Listen, Boone, I need to talk to you."

"Okay," I say. "Come on over now if you want to. We're just hanging out here. You know how to get to the new place, right?"

He doesn't say anything for a second and then says, "It'd be better if it was just me and you."

When I don't answer right away he says, "Give me a shout when you've got some time."

I start to say something and he just hangs up.

The first thing I think is, if he can't come around when Molly's here then the hell with him. That doesn't sit right, though, and I start wondering what has got him all tied up in knots like this. I mean, nothing ever gets to Tiny. The only time I've seen him even close to this was the morning of the fire up at his farm, the one that took out our still. That fire killed Jerry, too, but I think they decided he started it himself with that crack pipe. Carrie gave me all kinds of shit about that, trying to make it my fault that Jerry had gone back to using and ended up dead. She probably never got over that, and Mark said it was because she needed to blame somebody, and I was right there. I know she came into my house like a damn tornado that next morning, and if Mark hadn't been with her she might've swung on me.

Anyway, Tiny was so worried about his farm, all

the buildings and their house and all, that he was as serious as I've ever seen him. He worried about hot spots for days after it was out, even after we'd had a good rain.

All the rest of the time, even when I went after him that one time like a damn fool and he just wrapped me up and waited for me to get my shit back together, or when Nancy called him to help me out of that knife fight where Jerry was the only one with a knife, he was cool.

Nancy. As soon as I think about her, I'm thinking this has got to have something to do with him and Nancy. We've only seen them a few times since they stopped pretending they weren't together, and she still acts real uncomfortable around me and Molly, but even I can tell that she and Tiny are getting real serious about each other. It doesn't bother me, seeing them together, and I know it's because me and Molly have got it so good. I don't even care that they were sneaking around there at first, trying to keep me from finding out. It sure as hell bothered me then, when I figured out what was happening, but I didn't have Molly then. I look over at her, sitting in her chair, reading. She's pretty much always got a book either in her hand or in that little pouch on the side of her chair so she can get at it easy. I never knew anybody that loved books as much as she does.

She closes the book, reaches down to give Frankie

a scratch, and then straightens up and looks over at me. "What are you staring at?" she says.

"You're the best thing ever, you know that?"

She gets a little red. "What brought that on?"

I shrug. "Just thinking."

"I love you too, sweetie," she says. "You want me to give Gram a call, see if she needs anything? We ought to head that way before long, or we'll be late to the table, and you know how she is about that."

Sylvia doesn't need anything, and we get there in plenty of time to sit down and eat. Frankie and I stay until pretty late, and we get through the whole evening without talking about her moving or selling the house or me doing the right thing by Molly. It's still not like it used to be, though. All that stuff's just hanging out there, waiting.

A couple of days later I'm supposed to go look at a new job down toward Knoxville, and I give Tiny a call to see if he's going to be around.

"Sounds good. What time's your meeting?"

"The guy said 10:00, and I figure it won't take more than a half hour, an hour at the most. I'm going to have to tell him it'll be at least three weeks before I can get to him unless it's some little thing I can knock out in a day or so."

I tell him where I'm meeting the guy and he says, "You remember that burger place we went to just outside of Dandridge after we looked at one of those trucks you didn't buy?"

I have to think for a minute. "Yeah, barely."

"Meet me there and I'll buy you lunch."

"They have outdoor seating, right? I'll have Frankie with me."

"Pretty sure they do, but if they don't we'll get it to go and find a place on the lake that's got picnic tables and eat there. Maybe we'll do that anyway, more private that way."

"Tiny, what the hell's going on with you?"

"I'll meet you there around 11:30. Listen, I got to go. I'll see you tomorrow." I think I hear him start to say something else, but then he's gone.

I get to the restaurant about 11:20, and about 45 minutes later I'm ready to take off when I see Tiny's truck pull into the parking lot.

"You look like hell," I say when he gets out.

"Feel that way, too." He starts inside and turns. "You order yet?"

I shake my head.

"The cheeseburgers are really good. You want one for you and one for Frankie?"

"Yeah. No onion on Frankie's, but load mine up."

He comes back out with a big paper bag. "About ten minutes from here there's a boat ramp that's got some picnic tables off to the side. We better both drive. These folks don't like people using their parking lot unless they're eating here."

I have to pick the onions off of Frankie's burger, but I just add them to mine and we eat without either one of us saying much.

"Damn, I was hungry," he says. "You want another sweet tea? I got a couple of extra ones."

I shake my head. "Man, you want to tell me what the hell's going on here?"

He looks at me for a long minute. "Yeah. I got to tell somebody."

Then he just sits there staring out at the lake. Some guys drive in with a boat on a trailer, one of those sparkly things that probably cost as much as a house, and I can tell from how loud they are and how much trouble they're having backing the trailer down the ramp they've had a few already. One of them gets a cooler out of the back of the truck and passes it up to the guy up in the boat, and they get it in the water eventually and wait for the guy driving the truck to park the trailer. He gets closer than I like to our trucks and for a second I think he's going to scrape the side of Tiny's and I look over at him. He's not even watching. It's like he doesn't even hear all the noise or see what's right in front of him.

I stand up and Frankie does too, but the driver manages to miss both our trucks and heads down to the ramp, shouting at the other three guys to wait for him. They're laughing and giving him shit and acting like they're going to leave him, but he splashes out to the boat and they haul him in. They take off toward the main part of the lake, going like a bat out of hell, and about a half minute later I see a white boat with Wildlife Resources painted on the side come out from further up in the cove and head out after them. The two men in it are wearing some kind of uniforms, and I figure the three guys in the first boat are in a shitload of trouble if they catch them.

"So, anyway," Tiny says.

He's still staring at the lake.

"Anyway, Nancy calls me a couple of days ago and says she's pregnant."

He looks at me now, like he wants to see what I'm going to do or say.

First thing I think of is that talk me and Molly had about not being ready for kids. We've held on to that, but I got to say it's been pretty damn hard sometimes. I know I'm not ready to be a daddy, and I never thought about it until right now, but I guess I figured somebody like Tiny would be. He's always had his shit together like I never did.

The only thing I can think to say is, "So, y'all are going to have a kid?"

He's shaking his head. "Not if I can talk her out of it. I guess I'm the daddy, but, you know, I don't really know for sure. Never can tell about this kind of stuff."

"Damn, man, you think she was doing it with somebody besides you? I kind of thought you two were pretty serious about each other."

He shrugs. "I thought so, too."

I'm sitting here thinking, I bet he doesn't have anything to back up what he said. He just wants out of this. I feel like I used to know Nancy real well, and I can't see her going behind his back and screwing somebody else.

No. She wouldn't do that. At least I don't think she would.

"Have you talked to her since she, since she told you?"

He shakes his head. "Man, Stan is going to kill me if he finds out. He gets it in his head I've been screwing his little girl, he'll come after me, and he'll tell my folks, and spread it all over town, and . . . ."

It's like he runs out of stuff to say, and he's back to staring at the lake.

I wonder if he's thought about just taking off, moving somewhere else, and then I think, he can't really do that. He's got the money to, I bet, but he's got family here, and the farm, and lots of friends, and he'd have to leave all that behind. He'd never do it.

Before I met Molly it would have been easy for me just to take off if something like this happened to me. I didn't have family, or a home, or friends, or anything like that. Now I don't know if I could cut and run even if I wanted to, so it's for damn sure Tiny can't.

He's looking at me again. "What's New Orleans like?"

I'll be damned if he's not thinking about running off.

"So, you leaving?"

He looks down at the ground and then back up at me. "No. No, I can't do that. I'm just running my mouth."

He looks about as miserable as anybody I've ever seen. People always talk about how great it is to have a kid, it's the best thing ever, blah, blah. I can tell from these last few minutes Tiny's not feeling any of that.

"So, you ever do it with her?"

I shake my head. "No, never got that far. There was one time I thought we were going to, right after that fire up at your place, but we didn't. I think if we'd stayed together we would have, though, because her mom had just got her on the pill."

"She told me she was on it, and she doesn't know how it could have happened, but she says that sometime it does. I thought we were okay, man, I mean, I thought we were safe from this."

I don't know anything about all that. It seems to me like if you're taking the pill, you can't get pregnant, but to tell the truth, I haven't thought about it much. Molly, with what happened to Sylvia when she was young, just won't even take a chance and so far one or the other of us has been able to keep us from doing it.

"You're lucky, man, you know that?"

I look over at Tiny. "What do you mean?"

He shrugs. "I mean, Molly can't, right? She can't get pregnant because she's, you know, paralyzed."

I start to tell him he's wrong about that, and about Sylvia and what happened to her and that's why Molly won't even take a chance on getting pregnant. I start to, but it doesn't seem right, talking about Molly and Sylvia and their personal stuff. It's really none of his business, and it doesn't have anything to do with his problem at all.

He looks at me. "Right?" he says again.

"Man, I can't talk to you about me and Molly."

"Hell, Boone, I'm talking to you about me and Nancy."

I nod. "Yeah, and I don't know what to tell you about all that, either."

He stares at me.

"Hey, I'm telling you stuff here I wouldn't tell anybody else. I figured I could trust you."

I stare right back at him. "You and me, we've been through some stuff, so you already know you can. I can't tell you why it doesn't set right, talking about Molly, but it just doesn't."

He holds his stare for a minute and then nods.

"Okay, I guess I can live with that."

"And this thing with you and Nancy, I know that if I had something big like that I'd go see Mark. I don't figure you're going to want to do that, since you don't know him like I do."

He shakes his head. "It'd be like picking some random guy down at the grocery store and asking him what I ought to do."

I'm about to say something when I hear boats coming our way. Then the sparkly boat comes up to the ramp, moving real slow. There's two guys in it, and the other two are in the Wildlife Resources boat that's right behind them. One of the uniforms jumps out when they get close and wades in just ahead of the sparkly boat and grabs the rope that's tied to the front. He holds it while the two guys get out, get the truck, and back down to the ramp. They get the boat on the trailer and everybody just stands around for a few minutes. Then a van pulls up, and the four guys get loaded in, and the uniform pulls the boat out of the water and backs it into a corner of the lot. He locks the truck and puts a padlock on the trailer hitch. He gives the keys to the van driver, and it drives away. The Wildlife Resources boat picks him up and they head back into the main part of the lake.

Tiny watches the whole thing and then stands up. "I better get going."

I stand up, too, and grab his arm. He acts like he doesn't even notice and starts toward his truck.

"Hey, man, I got some more time if you want to hang out for a while."

He stops and turns around to face me. "No, I better get back home."

What are you going to do?"

"Damned if I know."

He starts toward his truck and turns around again. "You can't tell anybody about this, Boone. Not even Molly or Mark."

"Hell, I know that."

After he pulls out I gather up all the paper and stuff and throw it in the trash. "Come on, girl, let's get out of here."

Frankie hops in and we start toward home. All the way there I'm thinking about Tiny and the mess he's in. He's only got three choices that I can see. They can get married, he can talk her into an abortion or giving up the baby, or he can leave town. He really didn't talk about marriage today, so I figure that's not a choice.

I guess he's got a fourth one. He could stay, try to man up, and deal with all the shit from Nancy's family, his family, and all those rich people he's known since he was a little kid. I guarantee he doesn't like any of his choices. He's in a hell of a mess, that's for damned sure.

If Nancy had wanted to do it when we were together, I'd have said yes in a heartbeat, so I can't really fault Tiny. Hell, it wouldn't surprise me if it was his idea to start with and she said sure, I'm on the pill, we'll be fine. Or maybe if you asked them they wouldn't be able to tell you whose idea it was. Maybe it just happened.

Chapter Ten

A couple of weeks go by without me hearing from Tiny. I think about giving him a call, but I don't. I'm not sure what I'd say to him and I figure if he wants to talk to me some more he'll call me.

I try to think back to when I found out about him and Nancy. I don't usually pay attention to what day stuff happens or anything like that, but I'm thinking it's coming up on a year since I worked for Randy for a while. Looking back, they were for sure together before that, they were just keeping it a secret.

Damn, that means I've been with Molly for almost that long. It was right after Randy moved out of town that Sylvia called me to deal with those rosebushes.

"You know it's been almost a year since we met?" I say to Molly the next night, when we're getting ready to eat.

She nods. "I was thinking about trading you in on a newer model, but Gram talked me out of it."

Sylvia shakes her head. "Don't you believe a word

of that, Boone." She looks at me. "It was actually my idea to trade you in, and Molly wouldn't hear of it."

I'm usually the last one to get any kind of a joke, but this time I'm ahead of Molly, and I get to enjoy the look on her face before she figures it out. It only takes her a second, and she grins at Sylvia. "I'll remember that one, Gram."

We didn't joke at our house when I was growing up, so it's taken me a while to recognize one when I hear it. It was always real serious at home. We never knew what kind of mood Daddy was going to be in and Momma was, well, she was just there in the house with us. I can't imagine her telling a joke or playing a trick on anybody. The only one of us who did that kind of thing was Frankie, and after he died, nobody else even tried.

Plus, I caught a lot of shit from guys at school because I was a poor kid with a drunk for a daddy and no money or nice clothes, so pretty quick I got to where if anybody said anything to me I figured they were making fun of me. I got in more than a few fights because of that and, thinking about it now, I was probably the one that started about half of them.

I guess Gamaliel could joke around with me and I wouldn't get mad, but it took a while. Mark, well, Mark and I hit it off kind of from the start, and he's been able to kid around with me pretty much ever since we've known each other. The only other person

I've ever been able to go back and forth with, until I met Molly, has been Tiny.

I wonder if Tiny is okay and if he's figured any way out of this mess he's in. I almost reach for my phone and then I think, no, if he wants to talk he knows how to get in touch with me.

Most of the calls I get are either from Molly or somebody wanting some work done, so when I answer the phone a couple of days later and it's Mrs. Alder, I don't realize for a second who it is.

"Hello, Boone, it's Frances. I hope you don't mind me calling you out of the blue like this."

"No, ma'am, it's fine." I don't really know what else to say, so I just wait for her to say something.

"I wanted to let you know I've decided to get in touch with Natalie and Hannah, and I wanted to call you first. I imagine you'll be getting a call from them in the next day or so."

"I appreciate the call, ma'am."

She laughs. "Please, Boone, call me Frances. We are family, you know."

It feels weird, her being so old and all, but I remember Gamaliel did the same thing and we weren't even related.

"Okay, Frances. I got to tell you the last time I talked to Momma it was awful hard to hear. She was at work and it's a pretty noisy place. I'd tell you the best time to call, but, to tell the truth, I don't know when she's working and when she's off."

"That's okay, Boone. I think I'll wait until early evening. She works in a bakery, right?"

I nod and then remember I'm on the phone. "Right."

"Probably an early morning kind of work, so I think early evening would be best. Anyway, I won't trouble you any longer. I hope you and that lovely girl Molly are doing well, and say hello to Frankie for me."

"Yes ma'am, I mean Frances, I'll do that."

After I hang up, I realize I didn't ask why she had decided to go ahead and call. I wonder if she's getting sick or something.

"I'd say you're exactly right," Mark says when I call him. "I gave her your phone number the last time she and I talked, and if she reached out to you directly she probably had a good reason."

"She looked okay the last time we were down there," I say.

"I'm sure seeing you lifts her spirits."

I start to hang up when Mark says, "Have you wondered about the similarity between her first name and your brother's name?"

"Well, I'll be damned," is all I can think of to say. That kind of stuff just doesn't ever occur to me, but as soon as Mark says it I can see it.

Mark goes on. "She mentioned it in our last phone

call. It was something she was wondering about, too, and I think she'll be asking your mother about it, although probably not in the first call. Your mother needs to get past the initial shock of hearing from her before they talk about that kind of thing, and I'm sure Mrs. Alder realizes that. It may be just a coincidence, but if she and your mother were close, it would make sense.."

"She wants me to call her Frances. That felt a little weird before, but nothing compared to how it feels now."

Mark laughs. "I'll bet that's right."

"So, since Mrs. Alder, I mean Frances, and Hannah are both living in Middle Tennessee, Momma can go see them both on the same trip. If she's got a car or something." I hadn't even thought about that until now, but when Momma hears about her having a cousin she probably hadn't thought about in years, who knows what she'll do. She might quit her job and head this way. If she's got a car.

"Damn, Mark, this is going to shake things up for sure."

"No question about it, Boone."

I tell Molly and Sylvia all this the next day and Molly says, "Holy shit, Boone," and Sylvia looks at her and starts to say something. Then she looks over at me and shakes her head.

"That's not how I would have said it, Boone, but

this is certainly big news."

I nod. "I got no idea what's about to happen."

Then I say, "Oh, man. I need to call Mark right now."

Mark answers and I say, "Does Mrs. Cooperton know anything about all this?"

"I thought about that, Boone, and called Mrs. Alder. I told her she should explain things to Mrs. Cooperton first before asking to talk to Hannah, and she agreed that would be best."

I take a deep breath. "Good. That's good."

"Of course, Mrs. Cooperton doesn't have to let Frances talk to Hannah, and I would actually be surprised if she did. As far as she knows, Frances is just a stranger asking to speak to one of the children in her care. She will most likely refuse to call Hannah to the phone. In fact, Mrs. Cooperton may refer both Frances and your mother to the case worker in charge of Hannah's placement. If I were her, I think that's what I would do."

"Man, I am glad I'm not in the middle of this."

Two days later Momma calls me.

"Did you know about this?" She sounds really pissed off.

I start to ask her what she's talking about, but I'm pretty sure I know.

"Momma, you remember Mark, the preacher from the home I worked at?"

She doesn't answer.

"Well, he called me and said that Frances had gotten in touch with him because she thought she recognized me when I was working there. He said she wanted to talk to me, and so, yeah, I went down to the home she's staying in now and, well, it turns out she really is your cousin."

She's still not saying anything.

"So, she decided she wanted to get in touch with you, and Mark gave her your number. She's going to try to get in touch with Hannah, too."

She's quiet for another few seconds, and then says, "You should have told me, Boone."

"She wanted to be the one to tell you, Momma. I didn't see anything wrong with that. She's a real nice lady, and she was real glad to hear that you were out on your own, away from Daddy."

"Sounds like you told her a lot of stuff that wasn't any of her business." Her voice is ice cold.

I don't know what to say for a second, and I can feel myself starting to get mad. I take a couple of deep breaths and try to calm down.

I'm trying not to say anything about how she just left me to deal with Daddy all by myself and then, when she did come back, it was with that son of a bitch Jake and the only reason she came back was to steal my truck. So I tell her the same thing I told Inglewood, and then add a little. I just can't help it.

"Well, I didn't even tell her any of the really bad stuff, and if you don't want to see her I guess you can just not answer your phone the next time she calls."

I hang up before Momma can say anything else and when it rings again a second later I don't answer it.

I sure wish Molly was here.

Chapter Eleven

We're heading into fall for real now. A couple of nights ago it was in the high 40s, and I get two or three calls from people wanting me to rake their yards. The first one I go to is nothing but trees and it's probably close to half an acre. I have to space this job out because if it's windy, I get nothing done. The leaves end up right back where they were to start with. It takes me a week to do two day's worth of work. The second one's easier, but I'd rather go one on one with a copperhead than rake leaves.

"You did that already, and if I remember right you didn't like that much either," Molly says when I tell her how much I hate raking.

We're at my place having a couple of sandwiches and the last of a bag of chips, and I'm thinking an afternoon nap sounds pretty good when the phone rings.

Molly picks it up and says "Hello" without checking to see who it is. She gets a funny look on her face and says, "He's right here. Hold on just a second," and hands the phone to me. "It's Nancy," she says.

Man, I really don't want to talk to her. I don't know if Tiny told her that I know about her being pregnant, so I don't know what I can say without getting him in trouble. And I don't know why she'd be calling me anyway. Things have been weird between us ever since they ran into us down on Market Square in Knoxville.

Molly's looking at me and I shrug my shoulders like, how should I know what she wants, and take the phone from her.

"Hello," I say.

"Boone, where's Tiny?"

First thing I think is that he's run off so he won't have to deal with a kid, but I just can't see him doing that.

"I don't know, Nancy, I haven't talked to him in a few weeks."

"He told you about the baby, didn't he? He wasn't supposed to tell anybody."

She's talking so loud that, when I look over at Molly and see the expression on her face, it's pretty clear she's heard every word.

"Yeah, he told me, but he made me swear not to tell anybody, not even Molly, and I didn't," I say. "He said he had to tell somebody. It was eating him up, trying to figure out what to do."

"You've got to tell me where he is. I haven't seen him in three days, and he won't answer his phone. Please, Boone, you're his best friend. You must know where he is."

Damn. I never thought about being anybody's best friend, much less somebody like Tiny. I was a couple of years behind him in high school, but he was one of the popular ones. His family did those bonfires and just about everybody showed up at one time or another.

"I'm telling you, Nancy, I don't know where he is. I saw him a couple of weeks ago, and the last thing I said to him then was what are you gonna do."

"Well?" Nancy's crying, I can tell. "What did he say?"

"He said he didn't know."

She hangs up then. Just like that, she's gone.

I look over at Molly.

"That was awful," I say.

She nods.

"I mean, what the hell was I supposed to say to her?" I feel like I screwed that up but I'll be damned if I know how.

Molly doesn't say anything for what seems like a long time.

Finally she says, "How far along is she?"

I shrug. "Tiny didn't say."

She reaches out her hand. "Give me your phone."

I start to ask her why she wants it, but I don't. I just hand her the phone, and she calls the last number on it.

"Hello, Nancy? This is Molly. . . . No, he didn't tell me anything. I was just here in the room when you called him . . . . I know, I know . . . . I just thought you might need to talk to somebody, and since I already know . . . . sure, right now's fine . . . No, we're not there anymore. He had to move." She gives her my address. "See you in a half hour or so . . . It's okay, Nancy, really it is . . . Okay." She hangs up and turns to me. "Can you and Frankie go on a walk or something in about a half an hour?"

"Molly, what the hell are you doing?"

She looks at me and shrugs. "I'll bet she hasn't been able to talk to anybody, and so I offered."

"I didn't know you two were all that close."

She shakes her head. "We're not close, sweetie. She doesn't like me very much, and I get that." She smiles for just a second. "I'm sure she's got a lot of friends, she seems like the kind of person who would have. But they don't know about this, and she can't tell them." She's got tears in her eyes now. "Nobody should have to go through this by themselves."

I don't know what to say.

"So, can you two clear out of here? Be sure and take your phone so I can call you when it's okay to come back. She probably doesn't want to see any more people than she has to."

"Girl, you're a better person than I'll ever be," I say, and then, before she can do it, I say, "I mean woman."

She's still kind of teary eyed, but she laughs at that. "I'll get you trained yet, Boone. Now, you need to be out of here in fifteen minutes or so."

Sometimes I can barely stand to be around people I like, much less anybody else. I get what she's doing, but I know it's not something I'd be able to do, or would even think about doing. For her it was like a natural reaction.

It's a good two hours before Molly calls, and she says, "You know that pizza place we like so much? I'm calling in an order for a couple of larges and if you and Frankie could go pick them up in about fifteen minutes they ought to be ready."

"Two larges?"

"Nancy's going to eat here tonight. That's all right, isn't it?"

"Sure. You want me to get a six-pack?"

Molly says something away from the phone and comes back. "She says go ahead if you want to. She's not drinking, of course."

"Oh hell, I'm sorry, I didn't even think before I opened my mouth."

She laughs. "It's all right, really. All her friends

would have a beer if they were having pizza. That's one reason she's eating with us. She won't have to explain why she's having a Thunderstorm instead of a beer."

I pretty much get ignored all evening, which is fine with me. Nancy and Molly don't talk much either. It's like they're talked out, and they just want to have a pizza and relax.

Nancy gets ready to leave and squats down by Molly's chair. "You have no idea what this has meant, girl." She stands up and looks at me. "And you probably have no idea how lucky you are that she puts up with you. She's amazing."

I shrug. "I think she puts up with me so she can hang around with Frankie."

She laughs and then coughs a little. She wipes her eyes and says, "Wow. It's been a while since I heard anything I thought was funny enough to laugh at." She looks at Frankie. "Is that true, you beautiful girl? Are you the secret?"

Frankie wags her tail and Nancy laughs again.

"I'm going to get out of here. Thanks, Molly. Boone, if you've got half the sense I think you do, you'll hang on to her as tight as you can."

I know Molly's great, Mark's been telling me ever since he met her I need to hang onto her, and so has Raymond. Now Nancy just said the same thing, and I sure didn't expect that.

After she's gone I look at Molly. "I couldn't help but notice that she called you girl and you didn't say a word. You'd have been all over my ass if I had said that."

"It's different when it's just between us girls," Molly says, and gives me a wink.

Sylvia says she already ate and doesn't want the pizza we have left over, so I stick it in the fridge and take Molly home.

"You know, what you did for her tonight, that was . . . ," I start to say more, but I don't get to.

She pulls me into a kiss that goes on for a good long time, and when she leans back she says, "It's a good thing we're not back at your place. I'd get you into bed and never let you out."

"Sounds good to me," I say, "but what brought that on?"

"Give it some thought, sweetie. I'm sure you'll figure it out eventually. Now, if you'll help me into my chair you can escort me to the door and be on your way."

Chapter Twelve

Corey calls me a few days later and says, "I got a new job for you, and it's going to take a week or maybe a little more. How soon can you start?"

I look at my calendar and say, "It'll be a week and a half before I can start, but I've got a gap in there so I can give you a week and a few days if it takes that."

He doesn't like that, I can tell. After a minute he says, "I'll pay you for an extra two days if you can start middle of next week."

"Give me ten minutes and I'll call you back," I say, and he says okay.

"Well, Frankie, I guess it's a good thing I keep my jobs spaced out like I do. If I start this next job a day early, I can get on Corey by Wednesday of next week." I call to make sure I can move the job up one day and then call Corey back.

"We're good to go," I say.

"All right," he says. "You got a pen? I'll give you the address. Meet you there on Wednesday at about nine, and if you've got any cardboard boxes, newspaper, or blankets, bring them along."

"What kind of job is this?"

"There's a bunch of stuff we need to pack up that's breakable," he says. "When you get there you'll see what I mean. I'm going to be there by eight, so just look for my car."

I give myself plenty of time to find the place and end up getting there about fifteen minutes early. Corey is leaning against the hood of his car and waves me over.

"What did you bring?"

"Not much. I don't take the paper, but I brought some middle sized boxes and a couple of blankets."

He nods. "We'll be making more than one trip a day, so we'll reuse everything. I've got some stuff in the trunk. We'll haul it all out as soon as we figure out how to go at this."

I follow him in, and as soon as we get inside I can tell it's one of those buildings that's been added on to half a dozen times. He heads toward the back corner.

"Back in the first part of the last century, before they did all the adding on and the whole area got built up around it, this was an all purpose kind of place. General store, pharmacy, looks like some kind of government office like sheriff or something that got added later on. I got a deal on all the cabinets and whatever's still in them, but they're going to tear this place down starting in two weeks and put a godawful ugly big box something or other, I don't even know. That's why I had to have you as soon as I could. Let's take a look around and see where we need to start."

It takes the rest of the day just to figure out what we're doing. I've never seen Corey as excited as he is about this bunch of old cabinets and tables. He's talking half to me and half to himself. "We'll take this one just like it is, this one has to be unloaded. We better do the tables first, get them out of the way so we can work."

The next morning it's like he's got it all in his head about what to do and when, and we get down to it. The hardest thing is the pharmacy. I've never seen so many little glass bottles in my life, and some of them still have stuff in them. I get a box and some newspaper to start packing what's on the shelves and he stops me.

"You have to make a list of what's on each shelf and what order it's in," he says. "I want it to look just like this when we set it up, except the dust. And when we clean these bottles we'll have to be extra careful of the labels. I'm telling you, Boone, this is the best find so far."

By the end of the second day the tables are over at his place and we can work a lot easier. Corey takes charge of the pharmacy shelves, which suits me just fine. That's a lot of damn bottles, and he's real particular about it.

He puts me on the store shelves, and they come apart pretty easy. I get about a third of them on the truck for the first load and he says to take them on. "Just put them in that last empty section on the right as you go in," he says. "I'm not sure where I'm going to set up, but it'll be somewhere close to that."

He wasn't kidding about how long it would take. In a week and a half we get everything out of the old building so they can go ahead with the new whatever is going to be there, and me and Corey have everything spread over two spaces in his big building.

"I really appreciate this, Boone," he says. We're standing in the section of his warehouse where everything is piled up. "I needed that stuff out of that old building. I can probably handle it from here, but if you call me after your next job I'll let you know if I need any help putting this back like it was in its old location." He pulls out an envelope and hands it to me. "That's for two week's work."

"Thanks, man," I say.

"Glad to do it," he says. "You're a good worker."

This whole week and a half I've been expecting to hear from Momma, or Tiny, or Mrs. Alder, but the only person who calls me is Mark.

"How's everything?"

I can't tell him about Tiny and Nancy, or about Nancy and Molly, but I can tell him about Momma calling, and when I do he doesn't say anything for a few seconds.

"I'm very sorry how that turned out," he says, "but I'm not surprised. I got a phone call from Arthur and it was one of the more unpleasant calls I've had in quite some time. Evidently when Mrs. Alder called your mother it didn't go well, and she is pretty broken up about it. Arthur blames me, of course, but that's all tied up in our past history."

I know Mark said I didn't need to get in the middle of all this, but I feel like I'm being pulled in whether I like it or not.

"Do you know if Hannah knows what's going on here?"

Mark says, "That's one of the few bright spots in this whole mess. Mrs. Cooperton takes her role as a foster parent very seriously, and is shielding Hannah from all this. She doesn't even know that Mrs. Alder exists."

I nod and say, "That's good. What about Aunt Claire?"

"I don't think she knows anything about what's going on either. I'm certainly not going to add one more player to what is already a very complicated situation."

"So what am I supposed to do?"

"I would say nothing. You are an adult, so the issues facing Hannah don't apply to you. I would hope that your mother will soon realize you meant no disrespect by talking to Mrs. Alder. My advice to you is to continue to live your life with Molly and, if you are forced into this situation, deal with it then.

"Speaking of Molly, how is that lovely young woman you are spending all your time with?"

I try to think of what to tell him. What I really want to tell him about is what she did for Nancy because the more I think about it the more I think it may be the best thing I've ever seen. Since I can't, I say, "We're good."

This is starting to kind of piss me off. When Tiny said I had to keep this thing about him and Nancy secret, I said okay without even thinking about it. It hasn't even been two weeks and now it seems like I have a bunch of secrets to keep from the one guy I can always talk to instead of just one, and one secret I'm having to keep is that I can't tell him something really good about the woman I'm in love with. It's almost enough to make me break my promise to Tiny, but I can't do that.

So I kind of stumble around the rest of the time I'm on the phone with Mark, and I know he can tell something's not right. I'm just glad I'm not in his office. There's no way I could make it through without telling if he was sitting across from me.

I can still talk to Molly, though. Except when we're at Sylvia's. I'm pretty sure Molly hasn't told her about all this.

A couple of days later when I pick up the phone the number looks familiar, but I can't think who it might be. I answer, and it's Inglewood.

"Is this Boone?"

"Yeah. Who is this?"

"Arthur Inglewood. I'm in charge of the home where Frances Alder is a resident."

I don't say anything, and after a minute he says, "She wants to see you, insists on it in fact, but I wanted to call and lay out some rules before you come back. She's very upset about this, this issue with your mother, and I can't have you adding to that."

Damn, I wish Molly was here. I'd just hand the phone over to her and let her deal with this asshole.

"Does Frances know you're calling me and making up rules and stuff?"

"That's Mrs. Alder to you. I'll thank you to show a little respect."

"Well, she told me to call her Frances, so that's what I'm going to do. Not sure she'd like it much that you're calling me. Maybe you ought to check with her and call me back."

"I can't do that right now. She's actually not here. She's in the hospital."

Man, I hate hospitals. First my brother Frankie, then Gamaliel, and now Frances.

"Which hospital?"

He hesitates for a second and then gives me the name. "Don't make things worse for her, Boone. You and Mark have done enough harm already."

He hangs up then, I guess because he knows he can't keep me from seeing her if she's not even in his building. It's a good thing he did, too, because of that last thing he said about Mark.

I start to call the number and end up calling Molly instead. It's getting to where if I've got something going on the first thing I think of is to call her.

"Hey, sweetie, what's up?"

I tell her about my call from Inglewood and she says, "I don't think I would have done anything different if I was the one who got the call. Are you going to see her in the hospital?"

"I don't know, I mean, me and hospitals . . . ."

She's quiet for a minute, thinking. "Oh. I get it. Your brother. And Gamaliel."

"Right."

"Want me to go with you?"

"That's the only way I'd go, is if you were right there beside me."

"Okay. Just tell me when."

The night before we're supposed to go I call the hospital to make sure she's still there.

"Are you family?"

"I'm her cousin."

"If you want to see your cousin, you should come

soon."

When I say I'll be there tomorrow, the person on the other end says, "I'll let her know. What was your name again?"

"Boone."

"She mentioned you just the other day. I think she'll be very glad to see you."

The next morning I go over to Sylvia's and pick up Molly. Frankie is staying with her and Bert and Ray, and barely notices when we leave. She's too busy getting petted by Sylvia.

We get to the hospital in the middle of the afternoon, and I turn off the truck and sit there for a minute staring out the windshield.

Molly says, "You okay, sweetie?"

I shake my head. "I hate hospitals."

She nods.

"All right," I say after another minute has gone by. "Let's go see Frances."

I swear, whoever builds these things is trying to make sure people get lost. Every time I go into a hospital I'm mad before I even get to the room. We ask directions three different times before we get to the right floor. The door to her room is open about half way and I knock a couple of times and say, "Frances? It's Boone and Molly."

"Come in, please. I'm so glad to see both of you," she says, and I turn to Molly.

"She sounds pretty good."

Molly nods. "Let's go on in."

Frances is sitting up in her bed reading a book and puts it down when she sees us come through the door.

"What a nice surprise! I'm glad you made it. I'm not going to be here much longer." She sees the expression on my face and laughs. "Not because I'm dying, dear boy, although that day is coming soon enough. I'm being discharged day after tomorrow. It's just much easier here to visit without Arthur fussing around."

I nod and say, "Glad to hear you're going to stick around for a while."

"Me, too. Now," and her face changes, "have you heard from your mother?"

I nod again. "She was a little put out with me."

"I'm so sorry, Boone. I didn't mean to cause problems between you and your mother."

"Don't you worry about that," I say. "Momma and I have a lot of stuff we need to figure out. This thing with you, well, it's not the biggest thing we got between us."

She shakes her head. "If you'll forgive some unasked for advice from an old woman, make sure you clear things up with her. If you don't you'll regret it someday."

Molly has been listening and now she says, "I'll

keep reminding him of that, Mrs. Alder."

Frances looks at her. "Please, dear, call me Frances. I know I'm old, and calling me Mrs. Alder makes me feel even older."

Molly laughs. "Okay, Frances. I will."

The rest of the visit is pretty easy, maybe the easiest hospital visit I've ever had. She asks about Frankie, and the work I'm doing, and she and Molly talk about the book she's reading, and before I know it the nurse sticks his head in the door and says, "Visiting hours are almost over."

Frances waves her hand. "Okay, Gerald. I'll send them on their way shortly."

When he leaves she reaches for the book she was reading and takes three envelopes out from between the pages. She hands them to me.

"Your mother was a little put out with me as well, and, while I'd like to talk with her and maybe see her eventually, in case I don't get a chance to do that, I wrote her a letter. There's one for Hannah there, which you can give to her when it feels right, and one for you. You can open yours anytime."

She leans back. "Now. The nurses get less polite and more insistent the more times they come around, so I'll say goodbye now. It was a lovely visit, and I hope to see you again soon."

"Me, too, Frances, and I'll take care of the letters," I say, and as we leave I turn to look at her. She's back to reading her book. Gerald is on his way down the hall, checking rooms, and nods to us when we pass him.

Chapter Thirteen

I've just about given up on hearing from Tiny. It's been four weeks or so since we talked, so it won't be long before they won't have any kind of choice about an abortion. It may be too late already. I don't know about that. Tiny's always seemed like the kind of guy that doesn't run away from stuff, so I'm sort of worried about him. Maybe something's happened to him.

Nancy has been over to my place a couple more times, and it's almost like she and Molly are good friends now. Molly still runs me off, but I don't really mind. Sooner or later Nancy's going to have to tell folks about this, but until then Molly's all she's got.

It's the middle of the afternoon and I'm headed to the hardware store to pick up a couple of things when my phone rings.

"Hello."

"Hey, Boone."

"Hey, Tiny. Let me get to this parking lot right up

ahead so I don't have to try to drive and talk at the same time."

I pull into a fast food parking lot and find an empty space in the back.

"Man, where the hell are you?"

"I hear Nancy's been over at your place a few times. That right?"

"Yeah, she's over there right now. Molly always runs me off when she's coming over. Says Nancy can talk better when it's just the two of them."

He's quiet for a long time.

"So you're saying she's going over there to see Molly? I thought they didn't like each other much."

"Yeah, me too. Nancy called me looking for you a couple of weeks ago and Molly was in the room. She heard enough to know what was going on and called Nancy right back, invited her over." I stop for a second. "Wait a minute. You thought Nancy was coming over to see me?"

He doesn't answer.

"What the hell, man, are you drunk? There's no way I'd give up Molly for anybody."

I'm trying real hard not to get mad, but I'm having trouble with it. Then I think of something else.

"How do you know Nancy's been coming over? Are you in town? Following her around? Man, she's about half out of her mind wondering where you are."

He doesn't say anything.

"Hey, man, are you still there?"

"Yeah, I'm here."

What the hell am I supposed to do now? I know what I want to do. Tell him to man up and then hang up on him. I need to ask Molly or Mark what to do, but neither one of them are here. I got to figure this out on my own, and I don't like that one little bit. So I say the only thing I can think of.

"You hungry?"

He laughs that short laugh of his.

"Yeah, a little."

"Meet me at that same boat ramp we were at before. I'll buy the burgers this time."

After a minute he says, "Half an hour?"

"I'll be there."

When I get there Tiny's truck is parked over next to the picnic table. I've never seen it dirty before, but it sure is now. Tiny is sitting on the table with his feet on the bench. I park, grab the burgers and the drinks, and go over to him.

"I didn't think you could look worse than the last time I saw you, but I was wrong."

He grins, but it's not much of a grin. "Good to see you, too, Boone."

I hand him the sack and one of the teas. He stands up and steps off the bench.

"We eating here?"

"Sure." I'm kind of surprised at the question, but this whole thing is surprising me.

He sits down, opens the bag, and pulls out the burgers.

"Should be a large onion ring in there, too."

He takes the paper carton out, lays the bag on its side and smashes it flat, and pours the onion rings out on it.

His burger's pretty much gone before he says anything.

"I was almost halfway to Memphis before I, before I turned around."

"So you were leaving for real."

He nods. "Yeah. Damn coward."

I shrug. "You turned around, though, right?"

"Don't do that, Boone."

"Do what?"

"Try to make me out like I'm a good guy."

I'm no good at this shit. I know it.

"So, how long have you been back?"

He shrugs. "Couple of weeks. Maybe three."

I go back to the truck and get the other bag.

"They had these little fried pies. I got us two."

"Two each?"

I look at him and he's smiling. Or trying to.

"No, asshole, not two each. And before you ask, you can't have mine."

The pies are pretty good. They must be from a

fresh batch, because they're still warm. Tiny finishes his and stands up.

"Where are you going?"

He stands there for a second. "Don't really know."

I almost say you can come over to my place but then I think, if Nancy's still there I'm not sure I want to be anywhere in the same county when those two get together for the first time after what Tiny did.

"Look, man, you got to call her."

"I know."

"She's worried out of her mind."

"I know."

"And the baby—"

"Damn it, Boone, I know! I know, all right?"

"Listen, do you want to talk to Mark before you call her? Or Molly?"

He stares at me like I'm crazy.

"Why in the hell would I do that?"

I spread my hands. "You said a minute ago you didn't know where you were going, and I figure you're not real sure what to do, either."

"Yeah, maybe, but there's no way I'm talking to some guy I barely know, and sounds like Molly is all of a sudden Nancy's best friend. So unless it's you I talk to, man, I'm shit out of luck."

"You want me to tell you what to do? Man, I've barely got my own shit together on my best day."

"No, Boone, I know I got to figure this out on my

own. Just let me talk for a few minutes and if anything sounds real stupid, jump in. I've been talking to myself for the last three or four weeks and I just go round and round."

He starts talking, but he's barely into it when he stops. "Where's Frankie?"

"She's with Molly."

"You never go anywhere without Frankie. You must be dead serious about this girl."

"Woman."

"What?"

I grin. "Every time I call her a girl she corrects me. Must be working."

He shakes his head.

"Besides, we've been apart for longer than this," I say. "I left her with Sylvia when me and Molly went to see Frances over in middle Tennessee."

"Who's Frances?"

I tell him the whole story, starting with Mrs. Alder calling Mark and all the rest of it, including how it went down with Momma. He stares at me for a long minute.

"I don't know why I'm bothering you with my little problem. You've got your own pile of shit to shovel, don't you?"

I shrug. "It's working out. Momma's going to do whatever she feels like she has to, me and Frances are getting along fine, Hannah's in a good place, and

I've got Molly. I'm really okay."

As soon as I say that, I realize that it's true.

Chapter Fourteen

"I heard from Nancy yesterday," Molly says.

We're out driving around. I start another job in a couple of days, and we're just lazing through the afternoon.

"Oh, yeah?"

"Yeah. She said Tiny called her."

"Did he? It's about damn time."

"I agree." She pokes me in the side. "She told me he said you talked to him. Told him he needed to step up."

"Hey, don't poke at me like that. I'm trying to drive this truck."

"So when were you going to tell me that you talked to Tiny?"

I don't answer for a minute.

"I wasn't sure he'd call her."

"Well, he did."

"What did they get figured out?"

"I don't think they're that far along yet. She

knows they need to make some kind of decision, though. I think he knows that, too."

She stretches her arms out in front of her. "All I know is that I'm not in the middle of all that, and I can't tell you how relieved I am."

She reaches up to scratch Frankie's ear.

"I wonder if it's gotten back to Mark yet," I say.

"Why would it?"

"You know, Betty and Nancy's mom are good friends, Betty sees Mark pretty much every day. It just seems like the kind of thing that gets spread around, whether people want it to be or not."

"God, I hope not," Molly says. "Nancy will be so embarrassed. She and Tiny really need to get this figured out so they'll have answers for all the questions that'll be coming."

I don't say it, but I kind of hope it has gotten back to him. I'm not going to tell him, but if he already knows about it, I can talk to him without breaking any promises. I think I've been handling this whole thing okay, but I'd sure like to run it by him.

We ride along quiet for a while, and then Molly says, "You know what I think?"

"No idea, but I bet you're about to tell me."

She pokes me again. "I think I need to get a car. I'd like to start driving again."

"Okay," I say, because I don't know where this is headed.

"You know I told you about that place in Middle Tennessee that does conversions to hand controls? I might see if they've got a website. I'd like to know how much it costs to do something like that."

"So you won't need me anymore, right? I mean, if you can drive yourself."

"Oh, I might keep you around. I'm sure there's something you can do besides drive a truck," she says with a smile.

Two days later I get a call from Sylvia.

"You'd better get over here, Boone."

"What's wrong?"

"It's Molly. I'll tell you when you get here."

When I get to the door Sylvia opens it. "She's in her room. All she said to me was something about cars and money and then she went into her room. She's been there ever since."

I knock on the door and push it open a crack.

"Molly?"

No answer, but I can hear her crying.

"I'm coming in, okay?"

Still no answer. I step into her room and close the door.

She looks up when she hears the door close.

"How long have you been here?"

"About a minute."

She's propped up in her bed, looking at her wheelchair.

"You know what I said before about getting a car?"

I nod.

"Boone, are you even listening to me?"

I nod again and then say, "I'm listening."

"I found a place in Knoxville. I was looking for that place I got told about in Middle Tennessee and saw one real close by."

"That's good, right?"

She shakes her head.

"I called them today."

I wait for her to go on. I'm pretty sure I know what she's about to say.

"The guy I talked to said that it can't be just any car, that it has to be like a minivan and the whole thing has to be set up for handicapped people.

"The cheapest one is about thirty thousand."

Damn. That's way more than I thought it was going to be.

"And he said, he said," and she's starting to cry again, "he said the most expensive ones are more like seventy-five thousand."

She looks at me. "Where the hell could I get my hands on that much money?"

I shake my head. "I don't know, darlin'. I know I couldn't lay my hands on that much."

There's still a few thousand of Gamaliel's money in my safe deposit box, but it's nowhere near what Molly needs. I mean, I'd give it to her if it would make a difference, but it wouldn't.

She lays back in the bed, staring at the ceiling. "You know when I called Nancy?"

"Yeah."

"And I said if you want to talk anytime, I'll be here?"

"Yeah."

"You know what she said?"

"Not exactly."

"She said I'll be right over. You know why she could say that?"

"Because she's got a car?"

"Right! She's got a damned car!" Molly is still staring up at the ceiling, but now she's almost shouting.

"And you know why Ruby's not still wandering around the mall?"

At first I have no idea who Ruby is, but then I remember Sylvia's story.

"Because her nephew came and got her?"

"Right! Because he's got a damned car, too!"

I go over and sit on the bed next to her. I really want to say the right thing, but I'll be damned if I know what that is.

What I end up doing, or trying to do, is hold her hand, but she jerks it away. That pisses me off a little, because I'm just trying to help here, and I start to get up.

But I don't. Instead I lean over and scratch Frankie behind the ear. She's been sitting right next to my legs, and now she looks up at me like, "Aren't you going to do something?"

"I don't know, girl," I whisper. "I don't know."

Molly pushes herself up. "Did you just call me a girl? Again?"

"No," I say. "I was talking to Frankie. I always call her girl."

"Okay," she says, like she only half believes me.

"I swear," I say. "I even corrected Tiny when he said 'You must be serious about that girl.' I said 'Woman' and he looked at me like I was crazy."

"Really?"

I nod.

She smiles, just a little. "Well, okay, then."

I tilt my head toward the door. "You know, Sylvia's worried to death about you."

Molly rolls her eyes.

"She's always worried to death about me."

I stand up. "It's about time for her to start fixing dinner. Maybe I'll go see if she needs any help."

"She'll say no, you know that. She doesn't even let me help, except every now and then."

"Probably. You want me to tell her what's going on with you? She's going to ask."

She shakes her head. "I'll be out in a minute. I can tell her."

When she tells Sylvia about the call, she adds some stuff I hadn't heard yet. She says that the guy told her she couldn't just come in and pick up a car, that she would have to be evaluated by an occupational therapist. The OT would write a prescription for the kind of controls she would need, and the company would customize the car. Then she would have to be trained in how to use the controls before she could even think about getting the car.

After she finishes telling us about all that, she slumps back in her chair. "It's too much, Gram. Too much money, too much evaluating, too much everything." Her eyes fill up with tears again.

Sylvia looks over at me like she wants me to say something.

Trouble is, I'm pretty sure whatever I say is not going to make things any better. If I say it's okay, I can still drive her wherever she needs to go, we'll be back to the whole pity thing. If I agree it's not okay, that's not going to make her feel any better either. I take a deep breath and jump in.

"Hey Molly, how about if we start tomorrow looking around, see if we can find some way to beat that price? I can take on a few more jobs and put some money back, and we can go from there."

"I'm not taking any money from you, Boone," she says, and she looks kind of like she did when I told her she could move in with me.

"I wasn't thinking it would be a gift," I say, and shrug my shoulders. "I mean, you'd owe me."

Sylvia gives me a look, but I keep going.

"And I kind of like the idea of you owing me. We could work something out between us, you know, about making it right." I wink at her.

For a second I think I've really screwed up, but then I see a little smile.

"You think so?"

I nod. "Pretty sure."

When I look back over at Sylvia, I'd swear she's trying to cover up a smile of her own. She catches me looking and tries to be serious, but it's too late.

First thing I do the next day is call Mark, which is the first thing I always do when I've got a question I can't answer. This time, I'm not even sure where to start looking for an answer.

He wants a few days to think about it and maybe look around some. "We have people here who need all kinds of assistance, you know. Maybe somebody here knows something about what you need, or knows someone who does. I'll be in touch."

A couple of days later I'm finishing up a clean out job for a new customer when I get a phone call from Corey.

"You have some time in your schedule coming up?"

"Yeah, after I finish this one I've got a few days

before I start the next one."

"Come on up to the warehouse day after tomorrow. You'll be done by then, right?"

"What are we looking at?"

"Nothing right away, but I've been doing some work here and I might need you pretty soon."

Chapter Fifteen

Corey meets me at the door of the warehouse. "Let's walk through the place while I tell you what I've been thinking about."

He picks up a clipboard from a little table he's got set up right inside the door. He motions me over beside him and shows me the drawing he's made of the inside.

"Okay, I've got three bays on each side of this left hand aisle," he says, "so that's six, and the same on the other side. There's those spaces at the back, but I'm not counting them right now.

"So twelve in all, right?" He doesn't wait for me to answer, just goes right on talking. "I've been looking at what we've got in here so far, and almost all of it is from one time period. Between the wars." He looks at me. "And that got me started thinking about organization."

He starts walking, and I follow along. Frankie is right next to me, and we've been here so many times she doesn't even bother sniffing any of the stuff he's got scattered all over the place.

"I'm going to start organizing things this winter and that'll give me some idea of what to look for later on. What I want to do is recreate different scenarios from that era, using actual furniture and decorations, and so on.

"I've got this side marked on my plan as the city side. See, on the drawing I've got a bank, a pharmacy, a general store, a police station, a newspaper, and a post office."

We turn the corner and walk past the old car he's got sitting toward the back.

"My grandfather's car is too new to fit into any of these scenes, so I'll have to set aside a place for it. There's no way I'm getting rid of it."

We turn again, headed back toward the front.

"Okay, on this side, I'm thinking a farmhouse kitchen, a co-op, a barn and stables, a blacksmith shop, a toolshed, and I've got room for one more thing. Don't know what that's going to be yet."

"You going to have a tractor in here anywhere?"

He looks at me. "That's it! Perfect!"

He scribbles something on his pad. "None of this will have all the components, of course, just enough to give a sense of the time period."

We're back at the little table now, and he puts the clipboard on it and turns to me. "What do you think?"

I never understood why people wanted to do this kind of thing, hanging on to old stuff and then not using it for anything except to look at. All the stuff we had when I was growing up was old, but not real old, and usually in awful shape. I couldn't wait to get rid of whatever I didn't absolutely have to have. I know there are people who buy old stuff and spend all kinds of time and money fixing it up so it looks like it did when it was new, but I just don't get it.

Books are different, I guess, if you're a reader. Raymond has a big library, and I'm sure some of them are really old, but they read them. They don't just look at them.

So I don't really know what to say to Corey. I say the first thing that comes into my head, and it's because of what I was just thinking about.

"Sylvia would like to see something like what you're talking about putting together here, but Molly would wonder why you don't have a library on the city side."

"Who's Molly? And who's Sylvia?"

I might not have mentioned Sylvia to him but I'm pretty sure I've told him about Molly.

"Molly's my girlfriend, and Sylvia's her grandmother."

"Well, bring them by and we'll give them the grand tour. I'd love to talk to Sylvia about her childhood. Did she grow up anywhere around here?"

"I don't know, but I think so. She's been in the house they live in for a good long while."

"Great! Bring them by sometime. Just call me and make sure I'm going to be here."

He's real excited about this, and keeps me there for another hour talking about it.

"The only plan I had for this was preserving the beauty and feel of this area. I didn't know what it would look like, not really. I thought I was going to have trouble filling this thing up," and he waves his hand around, "but I can tell it's too small. When I got enough stuff in here to start seeing a pattern, the time period just jumped out at me, and now I can focus even more on what I want. I'm going to make a list as soon as I get what I've got in some kind of order and go from there.

"What I'll probably need from you for the next while is a day every now and then to move some of the bigger things and get them organized. I can do most of the final cleaning myself."

He looks around. "You know, if my grandpa hadn't left me that pile of money I'd still be teaching middle school. Not that I didn't love the kids, you understand, but this, all this, is just so much more fun."

He smiles a little. "I'm looking forward to when I can call my old principal and tell her that if she's got any field trip money, I've got something the older kids might enjoy."

"You know there's one thing," I say, "about me bringing Molly here."

"What's that?"

"Well, in here's fine, but out there," I point to the door, "you've got those steps coming into the small door, the one people use. And the threshold is pretty tall, too."

"So?"

"Molly uses a wheelchair, and she's not going to be able to get into and out of this building without a lot of hassle."

He stares at me.

"I mean, I don't know if you're planning for a bunch of people to come here and look at what you got, but it's something to think about."

After a minute he says, "Your girlfriend's a, a, I mean, she's in a wheelchair?"

"Yeah."

"Man, I am so sorry."

Something about the way he says that pisses me off, and I'm about to tell him he can take this fancy project of his and shove it when he steps over to the door. He looks out and then back at me.

"Can you bring her out here and have her take a look at this, tell me what I need to do to make it accessible for her?"

For a second I don't know what to say.

"I am so sorry, man," he says again. "I can't believe I never even thought about that. I guess since I don't have any trouble getting in and out, well, I just never thought . . ."

"Don't worry about it," I say. "We run into this kind of thing all the time. If you're willing to fix it, that's cool."

"When can you bring them out to see the place? We'll open the big doors and your girl, what's her name again?"

"Molly."

"Molly can get in and out that way, and she can show me the things I need to make right."

He shakes his head. "The sooner the better, okay? I'm going to feel bad about this until I do something about it."

I pull out my phone.

When Molly answers I say, "Corey wants you and Sylvia to see what he's been working on, and he says the sooner the better."

"Hold on a second." She calls out to Sylvia, "Hey Gram, Boone wants to know if we can go see the warehouse he's been working on with Corey. You have any plans for tomorrow?"

They're both good with tomorrow, so we decide on 10:30, and I figure we can pick up some lunch after we're done.

Molly thinks the warehouse is okay, but Sylvia

absolutely loves it. She and Corey take at least an hour to walk through the place, and it seems like they stop and talk about every other thing.

"Mr. Stinnett, I can't tell you how much I enjoyed your tour," Sylvia says when they finally get back around to the entrance.

"Please, call me Corey," he says.

"Of course, and I'm Sylvia. My mother grew up in the time period you're talking about here, and some of these things you've collected bring back memories of visits to my grandparents."

They're getting along so well Corey almost forgets to talk to Molly about the entrance. I'm about to remind him when he says, "Okay, before you folks leave, I'd like to get Molly's thoughts on how I need to change things here at the entrance to make this place accessible for everyone."

Molly points out the threshold and tells him the best place to add a ramp, and Corey writes it all down.

"I can't tell you how much I appreciate getting to meet both of you," he says. "I've got so many good ideas from this, and Sylvia, if it's okay with you, I'd like to have you help me with arranging some of the furniture in one or two of the displays."

When we get back to Sylvia's, I take the bag of sandwiches we picked up into the kitchen and she follows me in.

"What a delightful morning, Boone, and what a nice gentleman Corey is! He's very interesting to talk to, and this project of his is quite ambitious."

Molly is in the kitchen by now and says, "How did he come up with the money to build that huge warehouse and buy all this stuff?"

"Molly," Sylvia says, "that's really none of our business."

"I wondered about that too," I say, "but I never asked him about it. He told me yesterday he'd still be teaching school if his grandpa hadn't left him a pile of money."

"Well, he seems like a fine young man," says Sylvia. "We should eat. I believe our sandwiches are getting cold."

Chapter Sixteen

The three letters Frances gave me are sitting on top of the refrigerator. I don't know what I'm going to do about Hannah's, since she doesn't even know Frances exists, and I'm not sure about how to get Momma's to her. Maybe I'll wait until she calls me again, if she does, and I'll try to get an address early on in case we end up hollering at each other or one of us hangs up.

I take down the one she wrote me and carry it over to the couch.

For a minute I think about waiting until Molly is here, since she and Frances got along so well, but I decide to go ahead on my own. I really don't know why she felt like she had to write me a letter. Guess that's what old people do. I don't know anybody that writes letters.

I sit down on the couch and Frankie comes over and curls up on the floor beside me. Sometimes she would rather be down on the hard floor than be up on the couch.

The letter is on some kind of thick paper, real fancy, and Frances' handwriting is kind of hard to read because it's pretty fancy, too. I rest my elbows on my knees and start reading.

Dearest Boone,

I'm writing to you for several reasons. First, to say how glad I am that Fate brought us together. I must say I never expected to meet one of Natalie's children so late in my life.

Second, to thank you for being so kind to an old woman, near the end of her life, by making the effort to come see me and tell me about Natalie, and to introduce me to those with whom you are sharing your life. Your Molly is so special, and Frankie is just the best dog, but I'm sure you know all that.

But more than anything, I wanted to tell you about your mother. You knew her as an adult, and from what you have told me, one who was coping with a life that was difficult at best and filled with loss and pain. I knew a different Natalie.

I put the letter down on the couch beside me. Now I really wish Molly was here with me. I'm not sure I'm ready for whatever this is going to be.

The more I think about it the more I realize I

don't want to know what's in the rest of the letter, at least not right now. I know Momma's doing better now and all that, but she pretty much treated me like shit, the way I see it, and I don't think I want to know what a great kid she was.

I mean, she didn't beat me up or anything like Daddy did, and I get that Frankie dying just about killed her too, but she could have taken me with her when she took off. I would have gone in a heartbeat if it meant getting away from him. And she didn't have to come back here with Jake and help him steal the truck and never even try to see if I was okay.

Sometimes I think she should have stood up to Daddy, but then I don't know. He didn't mind hitting her, I know that, and he might have sent her to the hospital or worse if she'd tried to do something to protect me and Hannah.

But she could have gotten me out of there. And maybe before Frankie died she might have had the strength to, but after that she wasn't good for much of anything.

I think back to that weekend when she took off to Aunt Claire's and left me to deal with Daddy all on my own. Whatever it was set her off, it had to have happened after I went to bed, and it was enough to get her moving. I remember I never thought she'd get away from Daddy, and when I saw the note about getting Hannah ready to go on Monday I figured she wasn't coming back. I could have gone with Hannah. I could have.

Then it hits me that maybe Aunt Claire didn't want me. Maybe she said to Momma, you can come up here and bring Hannah, but Boone is just about a grown man. He can take care of himself.

Now I'm about as mad at Aunt Claire as I am at Momma. I don't guess I'll ever know if it was one or the other that didn't want me, or maybe it was both of them, but it makes me madder than I've been in a long time. Now I'm glad Molly's not here, and I'm pretty sure Frances never thought her letter would set me off like this or she'd never have written it.

The phone rings and it's Molly. "Hey, sweetie, how's it going?"

I don't answer right away and it's like she can tell something's not right. "Is everything okay, Boone? You know you can come over if you want to. It's a little late, but Gram would understand."

"I'd better not," I say, and I can hear how tight my voice is. "Let me call you back in a while."

"Sweetie, you're scaring me."

I shake my head. "Not trying to scare you. I just need to be by myself for a little bit."

"Okay," she says, but I can tell she's worried.

"I'll call her tomorrow, for sure," I tell Frankie. I fold the letter up and put it back in the envelope and take it over to where the other two are. I bet

Hannah's letter is a lot like mine, about what a great kid Momma was, but I have no idea what Frances would say to Momma. I'm real tempted to open the letter and see, but I just can't do it.

I make myself an S&S and sit around for a while, mad as hell at Momma and Aunt Claire for leaving me to deal with Daddy and just generally feeling sorry for myself. By the time I finish off my second one I start getting tired of feeling like this and say to myself, "So you got shit on, Boone. So what? You were a kid, shouldn't happen to a kid, blah, blah, blah. You're a grown man now, and you better start acting like one."

That works for a few minutes. Then I'm right back into feeling sorry for myself.

The rest of the evening goes back and forth like that, but the next morning I'm doing a little better. Frankie and I run a couple of errands, and we get back home about an hour before lunch time. I give Molly a call to see if she wants to go somewhere and get a bite.

"Are you okay, sweetie?"

It takes me a second to remember how we left it last night.

"Oh, yeah, I'm good. Last night I tried to read that letter Frances gave me and ended up most of the night feeling sorry for myself. Stupid kid stuff. One of these days I'll go back and read the rest of the letter, but not going to do that anytime soon."

"Why, what was so bad about it?"

I knew she was going to ask that, and I really don't want to talk about it right now.

"Reason I called was, I was wondering if you wanted me to come by and pick you up and we could go to that place down in Knoxville you've been wanting to try. You know, get some lunch?"

"You told me you weren't interested in Mediterranean food, remember?"

"Maybe they'll have a burger or some chicken strips or something."

She laughs. "Okay, but you might change your mind once we get there."

The place is right in the middle of downtown and I'm wishing I had one of those handicapped tags to hang on the rearview mirror. We circle two or three times, trying to figure out all the one-way streets and finally somebody pulls out of a spot almost a block away. She had pulled up the menu on her iPad before we left and says she's going to get a sandwich made out of falafel, whatever that is, and I decide to try a sandwich that says gyro on the menu. No idea what I'm getting into but I figure, what the hell.

On the way to the restaurant we decide to get the food to go and take it over to Krutch Park, which is real close by. I haven't been there since that time we saw Tiny and Nancy, back when they were pretending they weren't a couple. That seems like a long time ago. I let Molly take care of the ordering and Frankie and I wait for her on the sidewalk.

I got to say, the gyro is really good. It's a roll up sandwich and there's a sauce on it I've never tasted before. It's pretty messy to try to eat it, but damn, it's good. Molly let me try her falafel and I think the gyro's way better, but hers is not bad.

"Next time we'll get the spicy ones," she says.

After we finish she says, "So, you want to tell me what you were so upset about last night?"

I shake my head. "Not really."

"Okay."

"I don't want to because I was acting like a big damn baby and I'm kind of embarrassed about that."

I'm bent over scratching Frankie's ear, trying not to look at her, so I don't see her turn towards me.

"You don't need to worry about me, Boone. I'm not going to make fun of you. Don't you know that by now?"

I've spent a lot of my time assuming that I'm being made fun of, and back when I was in school I would have been right a lot of the time. Here I am four or five years out and it's still hard for me to see that somebody, even somebody like Molly, is not going to make fun of me.

The thing is, even when Molly or Mark, or even Tiny, does say something it doesn't bother me, at least most of the time. Some of the stuff they say, if anybody else said it I'd be right up in their face. I can hear it from one of those three and we all end up laughing about it.

"Yeah, I know," I say, and I tell her about what was in the only part of Frances' letter that I read, and how I ended up thinking about Momma and what she didn't do to take care of me back then.

"You see why I didn't want to tell you?" I say. "I get started thinking about that stuff and it's like I'm a little kid all over again, and it's real hard for me to pull myself out of it. I ought to be past all that by now, I mean, I'm a grown man. It pisses me off when I catch myself acting like I'm still in high school."

"Actually, Boone, you're not all that far out of high school," Mark says the next day. The three of us are in his office and Mark is leaning back in his chair. Molly's got her eyes on Mark and Frankie, as usual, is pretty much ignoring the whole thing.

"I told him he's got it together a lot more than most of the people I know from school," she says, "but I got the feeling he thought I was just trying to make him feel better."

Mark nods. "Not that there's anything wrong with trying to make somebody feel better, but I agree with you. Our friend Boone, most likely due to what has been required of him the last few years, is in pretty good shape for a man in his early twenties."

She looks over at me and then back to Mark. "Barely in his twenties. Sometimes I think he only likes me because I'm an older woman."

Mark laughs out loud and even I have to smile a little bit at that. He shakes his head at me. "How in the world do you keep up with her?"

I shrug. "I don't even try."

Chapter Seventeen

A few days later I'm finishing up one of those little jobs that I can pretty much do in my sleep when I get a call from Tiny.

"Hey, Boone, you in the middle of something?"

"Just finishing up a job, take me about another half hour."

"I thought maybe you and Molly might want to go get something to eat. Nancy and I've been thinking about that new Italian restaurant that opened last month. It's kind of in your direction and we checked already about it being good for Molly to get into and move around, you know, so unless you've got something already, we were thinking tonight about seven."

"Far as I know we're good. Let me call Molly and I'll get back to you in just a minute."

I call Molly. "You're not going to believe who just called me about going out to eat."

"Tiny, right?"

I don't say anything and she laughs. "I'm not a mind reader, sweetie. Nancy called me about two minutes ago."

"So you want to go eat some Italian food?"

"You bet I do. Sylvia said she'd watch Frankie for us, and Nancy said they were thinking around seven. Does that give you enough time to finish up?"

"I'm only a half hour or so from being done. I'll call Tiny and tell him we'll meet them there at about seven."

When we pull out of Sylvia's driveway I look over at Molly. "So what happened with Nancy and Tiny? I didn't have any idea they were even talking to each other. I mean, you told me Tiny finally called her, but that's all I knew about."

She shrugs. "Guess we'll find out." She looks over at the passenger door. "Feels strange not to have Frankie along. Want me to scoot over and give you some more room?"

We come around a curve and the road straightens out. I put my arm around her shoulder and say, "You're fine right where you are."

When we get to the restaurant Tiny and Nancy are already there, waiting for us out on the sidewalk.

"There's about a ten minute wait," Nancy says. "We got our name on the list and told them what we needed." She looks at Molly. "The hostess acted like she was a little put out. You run into that a lot?"

"Depends," Molly says. "We've got a couple of places that we go to pretty often, and they're real nice. Some places, the first time's a little tense."

Tiny shakes his head. "That ain't right, man." He looks over at me. "You used to have a little bit of a temper, if I remember right." He doesn't say anything else, but we all know what he's talking about.

I grin. "Almost had to kick an ass or two, but Molly told me she'd stop letting me take her out if I didn't learn to behave myself."

Tiny looks at Molly. "You must be doing a good job getting him trained. I can remember a time when you couldn't take him anywhere."

I'm about to say something when the buzzer in Tiny's pocket goes off and we head inside.

When we were growing up I used to wonder what it would be like to be able to go to a Krystal or McDonald's whenever I wanted to. We never went out to eat, because we never had the money to. This restaurant is pretty nice.

The waiter comes around and asks what we want to drink. "I'll have water with lemon," says Nancy. The waiter turns to Tiny and he looks kind of uncomfortable until Nancy says, "For goodness sakes, Tiny, go on and order a beer. You know you want one, and I don't mind. Really I don't."

Molly and I each order a glass of red wine and Tiny says, "Well, look at you two getting all fancy.

You trying to make me look like a redneck, Boone?"

I start to answer and Molly says, "It's Raymond's fault, Tiny. He and Charlotte are corrupting Boone something awful."

"Who are Raymond and Charlotte?" Nancy asks.

I look at Tiny and he says, "I never told her hardly anything about your trip, so you'll have to start from the the time y'all met."

I tell Nancy about meeting them down in Georgia and what happened down there, and how they're just running around all over the country in that big RV. When I tell about our two weeks up at their place in Virginia Tiny says, "When did you go up there? I didn't know about this last part."

"Back in the summer. Late summer, I guess," says Molly. "You should see their library."

We tell them about the little cabin on their property where we stayed, and about Raymond's plans to get Molly back up there to work with him on a trail that she can use when he starts on his plans to landscape the fifty acres they've got.

"Damn, son, you're moving in some high circles," says Tiny.

"Right place, right time. If those assholes had pulled in two minutes later me and Frankie would have been gone already."

The waiter comes up and takes our orders. Tiny says he's heard the lasagna is really good, so he orders that. Nancy says, "I'm just going to have a salad, and maybe a bite of your lasagna."

He looks over at me. "Molly do that to you?"

"I don't know what you're talking about, man."

I've been looking over the menu and when the waiter comes over to me I point to the fettuccini alfredo and say, "Tell me what this is."

He looks at me like I must be stupid not to know that already, and I'm about to say something when Molly says, "I love fettuccini alfredo, sweetie. Let's split that and get a couple of salads. That way we'll have room for dessert." She smiles up at the waiter. "Can we get an extra plate, please?"

When he's gone I say, "Boy, I'm glad you jumped in there, darlin'. I didn't even know how to say that. Probably would have called it Alfred."

Tiny's grinning at me, and when I look across the table he nods. "Yeah, I saw a little flash of the old Boone there for a second. Molly probably saved your ass from being thrown out of here. I mean, if you had jumped the waiter because you thought he was about to laugh at you."

"One of my many talents," says Molly. "Keeping Boone out of trouble."

I don't tell them, but about half the time I still feel like the old Boone. I'm pretty sure if I didn't have Molly I'd be mad a lot more of the time. She's good for me, that's for sure.

"Boone, you're a thousand miles away," Nancy says. "What's going on?"

About that time the salads show up and I say, "I'm thinking that if I don't get something to eat pretty soon I'm going to fall out of my chair. I'm a working man, you know."

Nobody at the table believes me, but since the food's right there in front of us we dig in.

The fettuccini alfredo is real good, and there's a lot of it. I still want dessert, though, so me and Molly split something called a cannoli cake that just about fills me up.

We're finishing up the last of the cake when Tiny says, "I'm real glad you guys are here."

He reaches over and puts his hand on Nancy's. "I'm not sure I'd have the nerve to go through with this if, well . . . ." He reaches in his pocket and pulls out a little black box.

As soon as Nancy sees it she starts crying, and when I look at Molly she's about to cry, too.

Tiny looks at Nancy. "I know we've sort of talked about this maybe happening sometime. If you'll have me, I'd like for it to happen now." He opens the box and takes out a ring. "Hope it fits."

Nancy holds out her hand. It's shaking so bad Tiny has to grab hold of it to steady it enough to slide the ring on. "What do you think?"

It takes her a minute to get herself back together.

"I think we need to go tell my parents."

Then she turns to Molly. "Oh my God!" and she starts crying all over again, and now Molly is too, and I look over at the next table and the couple there are smiling big smiles.

"They already know," says Tiny. Nancy takes a deep breath and looks over at Molly.

"How is Stan?" I say. Tiny gives me a look and I figure I've said something wrong, but he shrugs his shoulders and says, "About the same. Actually, when I told him I wanted to ask Nancy to marry me he was about as happy as I can remember ever seeing him." He turns to Nancy. "He hollered for your mother and told her, and she's probably still crying."

"Oh, I'm sure," says Nancy. She's staring at the ring. "It's so beautiful."

Molly asks about the date and Tiny says the sooner the better. Nancy nods, and I see her lay her hand on her stomach for just a second.

The waiter comes over with the check and I start to pull out my wallet. Tiny says, "This one's on me, Boone. You bought the last time, remember?"

"If you're talking about those burgers and onion rings, then I think I'm still going to owe you," I say, but I put my wallet back. "Molly told me it's bad manners to refuse a gift, so, thanks."

"See?" says Molly. "Still working on him. He's a good student, but has a lot to learn."

I nod. "What can I tell you? When she's right, she's right."

Nancy and Molly head off to the restroom and I look over at Tiny.

"So, you ready for this?"

He shakes his head. "Not even close."

I nod. "I get that. But Nancy's a great girl, man. I'm real happy for both of you."

"I thought about getting a place somewhere, like Knoxville or Greenville, and we could just move in together, see if it would work out, but Stan and my mom would gang up on us if I tried that. So then I thought maybe just run off somewhere and get married, call her folks later and tell them, but I know Nancy wants a big deal wedding, so I guess that's what we'll have."

"She didn't know you were going to do this tonight?"

"I think she knew it was coming sooner or later, the way we've been talking."

On the way home Molly is real quiet.

We're about halfway to Sylvia's when she says, "What did you think about all that?"

I glance over and back to the road. "I guess it's good. I mean, if she's going ahead with having the kid, it's the right thing for Tiny to do."

She doesn't say anything.

"Right?"

After a minute she says, "I guess so. I don't know, sweetie, I always thought getting married is something you do because you want to, not because you feel like you don't have a choice." She gets quiet again and then says, "You know?"

We ride along for a few miles and I say, "So have you ever thought about getting married, you know, sometime?"

"Sure, I mean, I don't know if it's ever going to happen, I mean, with me in this chair and all."

"If I was to think about marrying somebody, I sure wouldn't let a chair stop me."

The words are out of my mouth before I even think about them. What I'm thinking is, I'm real glad that I'm not going to have to make the kind of choice Tiny just had to, and if me and Molly get married I'll be a lot happier than it seems like Tiny is right now. He kind of acts like he's in a trap he can't really get out of.

I glance over at Molly again. She's real still, staring straight ahead.

"I mean, if I had my shit together a lot more than I do, I might think about getting married."

She makes a noise. "Please, Boone, you've got it together more than most people."

I don't see how anybody could think that. Not if they knew how sometimes it's all I can do to keep my mouth shut, or knew half of the really shitty things

I've done in my life.

"Well, I don't know about all that," is all I can think of to say.

"Oh, sweetie, if you go on thinking like that then we'll nev—" she stops right there and takes a deep breath. "Sorry. Sorry."

"What?"

"Nothing."

She doesn't say a word the rest of the way to Sylvia's and when we get to the door she says, "I guess I'll see you later."

"I'll call you tomorrow."

"Okay."

This feels wrong, like Molly's disappointed in me, and I got to say this has been the weirdest night I've had in a long time. Tiny didn't seem all that happy when it was just him and me. I wonder how Nancy is, but it doesn't seem like I ought to ask Molly about that. At least not right now.

"I better get Frankie."

"Oh," she says. "I guess you better."

We go in and Sylvia's in her favorite chair in the sunroom with a book in her hand, but she's about half asleep and she gives a little jump when she hears us come in.

"Didn't mean to wake you up, Sylvia, I just need to get Frankie out of your way."

"How was the restaurant?"

"The food was real good, Gram. Boone just came in to get Frankie and he's got to get going. I'm going on to bed. See you tomorrow."

Molly's out of the room and Sylvia's still trying to wake up.

"Is everything all right, Boone? Did you two have a fight?"

I shake my head. "I'm not sure."

On the way home I go over the whole thing with Frankie, from the time we left the restaurant until I picked her up, and decide that it wasn't a fight. I kind of wish it had been. Whatever this was, I don't think a fight would have felt this bad.

Chapter Eighteen

For the next week me and Molly have a hard time with just about everything. When we talk it's like we almost understand each other, but not quite, and we each have to make sure we know what the other person meant. It's driving me crazy because it used to be so easy with her, we'd just say a word or two and get it. Wouldn't even have to finish the sentence.

I don't find out it's bothering her as much as it is me until this evening when I come into the room where Sylvia and Molly are, and they're talking. They shut up as soon as they see me, but the last thing I hear Sylvia say is, "Just tell him, dear. I do hate to see you moping around like this."

Molly turns her chair around and says, "I'll be back in just a minute," and she's out of the room before I can say a word.

Sylvia shakes her head. "I'll be glad when you two get this worked out, whatever it is. I hate to see you tiptoeing around each other like this."

As soon as she says it, I think, that's exactly what we've been doing. Tiptoeing.

"Excuse me for just a minute, Sylvia," I say.

When I get to Molly's door I start to knock but then I think, what the hell, and I push the door open.

Molly is sitting in her chair just staring at the wall. She looks up at me and says, "You're supposed to knock, you know."

"Yeah, I know."

After a minute she says, "So what do you want?"

I look at her. She's the best thing that's ever happened to me, and I can't even think of the right thing to say.

She lets me stand there like a damn fool for what seems like a long time before she says, "So you don't want anything?"

My phone rings and I decide to leave it in my pocket, but after the third ring Molly says, "You'd better get that."

I pull it out and say, "Hello."

Mark says, "Hey, Boone, are you working on a job right now?"

"No, I just finished one yesterday. You sound like something's wrong. Is Hannah okay?"

"Hannah's fine," he says. "I had a long talk with your mother today, and if you've got some time tomorrow, I'd like to buy you lunch and tell you about some of the stuff she said."

I'm not real sure I want to hear anything about Momma, but Mark doesn't ask all that often.

"Yeah, I can come down tomorrow," I say. "If Momma told you something you think I need to hear, how come she didn't just call me?"

"That's part of what I want to talk to you about. See you tomorrow," and he hangs up.

I turn to see Molly watching me.

"That was Mark."

"I figured that. What's going on?"

"I'm not sure. He wouldn't tell me over the phone. I got to tell you I'm kind of worried."

She doesn't say anything, and after a minute I say, "Well, I guess I'd better get out of here."

I turn toward the door and she says, "Boone, listen, I . . . ."

"It's okay," I say. "You wanted to be by yourself and I came busting in here, didn't even knock. I'll call you after I talk to Mark."

Mark is in the parking lot when I pull in. He comes up to the truck and says, "It's a warm enough day to eat outside. Want to go to the same place we ate last time?"

I nod. "We'll follow you."

He looks past me. "Where's Molly?"

"It kind of sounded like you·wanted to talk to just me." I know how lame that sounds, and I'm pretty sure he does too.

"Okay," he says.

The place is busy, but there's a table off to the side and we order from the same waitress we had the last time. She remembers Frankie.

"Hello, you beautiful girl! Is he being good to you?"

Mark laughs. "He treats Frankie better than anybody else, including himself."

She leaves and I say, "What was that supposed to mean?"

He gives me a look. "Just a joke, Boone. What's wrong?"

I start to say nothing, but I know better than to try that with Mark.

"Me and Molly are kind of weird right now. I mean, ever since that dinner when we found out that Tiny and Nancy are getting married . . ."

As soon as the words are out of my mouth I think, oh shit, I bet that was supposed to be a secret, like her being pregnant.

I look over at Mark. "Sorry. I don't think I was supposed to say anything about that."

Mark didn't know, I can tell by the look on his face. "Well, this is kind of unexpected," is all he says.

I don't say anything, but he's watching me and all of a sudden he says, "How far along is she?" and I say, "I'm not sure," and I'd give anything to have that back but it's too late.

He leans back and says, "Oh, boy."

"Listen, Mark, I swore I wouldn't say anything about any of this. Don't tell anybody, okay?"

"Of course. We'll pretend I'm a preacher and you told me this in confidence." He grins.

"Thanks, man," I say. "I really need to talk to you about all that, but I guess I need to hear about Momma, too."

"I don't have anything this afternoon, Boone. We can spend as much time as you need."

I tell him the whole story about Nancy looking for Tiny, me thinking he had left town, and about them surprising us with Tiny proposing at the restaurant and how weird the whole thing felt.

What Molly did, reaching out to Nancy when she found out about the pregnancy, really got to Mark, same as it did me.

"She is the embodiment of the Good Samaritan story," he says.

Not real sure what embodiment is, but I can guess. "She's an amazing woman," I say.

"That she is," says Mark. "So what's the problem between you two?"

I tell him about us talking on the way back from the dinner and what I said about not having my shit together enough to think about marrying anybody.

"I mean, if I thought I could get it right, I'd ask Molly tomorrow," I say.

He's shaking his head. "Boone, nobody is ever

really ready for a step like that, even those people who think they are. Imagining what marriage is like and experiencing the reality of it are two different things entirely."

I'm pretty sure Mark's never been married. I mean, there's no ring on his finger, no pictures in his office, no stories about him having a wife. I start to ask him what makes him such an expert, but I figure he's seen enough in his job to know a hell of a lot more than me.

"I think that's what's bothering Molly," I say. "When I said that, it was like she pulled away from me. She didn't move or anything, but, you know what I mean?"

He nods. "I've seen you two together, and I don't think I'm going too far out on a limb to say that both of you want this to happen eventually. How long has it been since you were at the restaurant with Tiny and Nancy?"

When I tell him a little over a week he says, "I'd say give it a little more time and things may get back to being comfortable. They won't ever go back to the way they were before. I think you know that. Two of your friends have made a significant change in their lives, and there's no way that won't affect the two of you."

I think about it for a minute. I can't even imagine not having Molly around, but if I asked her right now it'd be kind of like me copying Tiny, and I don't want to do that. Me and Molly are coming up on our second Christmas together, and that's still a little ways off.

"Maybe I'll get her a ring for Christmas."

"There's a long tradition of taking advantage of a holiday for things like that. I think Tiny and Nancy were forced into a decision by circumstance and you and Molly don't have that ticking clock to push you into something."

Even though he's right, like he usually is, it still doesn't make me feel any better. I know when Tiny pulled out that ring at the restaurant and asked Nancy, it made me think about asking Molly, and the first thought in my head was, what if I ask Molly and she says no?

Thinking about this scares the hell out of me.

"So what's Momma got to say that she couldn't tell me?"

I don't know if talking about Momma is going to be any better, but I got to change the subject.

Mark waves at the waitress. We'd finished our lunch a long time ago and the place is almost empty. She comes over and says, "You two need the check?"

Mark shakes his head. "I was thinking I'd like a cup of coffee, if you've got some fresh." He looks over at me. "Boone?"

I nod.

"I'll make a pot," she says. "We usually do about

this time of day anyway, mostly for the staff. But I guess we can share with you guys."

She goes off to make the coffee and Mark says, "Your mother has been afraid to call you, she says, because last time you hung up on her." He gives me a look. "Is that right?"

"More or less," I say, and tell him about how she was all over me because I talked to Frances about what it was like at our house when I was growing up.

"And, like I told her, I didn't even tell Frances the bad stuff. Plus she's family, so I didn't think it was that big a deal."

The waitress comes with two cups, and we sit for a minute sipping the hot coffee before Mark puts down his cup.

"That's not exactly what she told me about what happened, but it's close enough," he says. "If I were to guess, I'd say that she really looked up to Frances when she was growing up and was more than a little embarrassed for her to find out what a difficult life she had led."

"Yeah, but she's out from under now."

He nods. "She is, and from what I could tell, kind of reading between the lines, she's still doing well overall." He takes another sip of coffee.

"If you're getting ready to tell me I need to call her up and apologize, that's not going to happen."

"If this was three or four years ago, that's

probably what I would do," he says, "but you're a different person now. You've matured quite a bit from when I first met you, Boone, and I trust you to make that kind of decision at your own pace."

He's like the opposite of Momma and Aunt Claire. They would be pushing hard and wouldn't let up until I gave in. I appreciate him laying back like that, but I'm getting a little tired of people telling me I've really got it together. I don't believe I do, so it makes me think they're after something.

"She wants me to call her after I talk to you," Mark says. "You want me to give her a message?"

I get a little mad about that, that he's reporting back to Momma, and I'm about ready to say it looks like Inglewood is right about him loving to stick his nose into other people's business.

The only reason I don't is I like Mark, and I don't like Inglewood, and I really don't want to say they're the same at all. Or even think it.

"No," I say. "I don't have a message for her. If she wants to call me she can."

"If I were to tell her you're glad she's still doing well, would that be the truth?"

"Listen, man, I don't want you or anybody else putting words in my mouth, okay?"

He holds his hands up. "Okay. I know from what you've told me there's a lot to work out between you and your mother. I won't add to that by guessing how you're feeling."

I've had about all of this serious talk I can stand, and I think Mark figures that out, because he waves at the waitress and asks for the check.

Chapter Nineteen

When I walk into the sunroom Sylvia is sitting there holding a letter. Molly goes straight over to her and puts her hand on Sylvia's arm. "Gram, Boone's here."

She looks up. "Oh, Boone, I'm glad you're here. This," and she waves the letter at me, "came in the mail yesterday."

I don't know what it is, but from how serious everybody is I figure it's something important.

Things with me and Molly have been better the last week or so, but they're still not right. I look over at her and she's staring at me, which is something she hasn't done in a while. Lately when I catch her looking at me she turns real quick. Not this time.

"Gram got a letter from The Commons," she says.

With all the other stuff going on, with Tiny and Nancy, and Momma and Frances, I had forgotten about Sylvia's move. As far as I knew when I first heard about it, it was a year or more off.

"Boone, would you have a seat? Can I get you a glass of wine?" Sylvia stands and sets the letter on the table beside her chair.

I shake my head.

"I believe I'll have one."

"Me, too," Molly says. "I'll help you, Gram."

I sure would like to know what the hell is going on here. They're both acting awful strange.

When Sylvia is back in her chair she says, "You know that not long ago, I put my name on the list for a spot at The Commons."

I nod.

"At the time I was told the waiting list was over a year long, so I never gave it much thought after that," she says. "Yesterday I got this letter, and as it turns out, they expect to have a place for me in about three months."

I'm afraid to look at Molly, so I keep my eyes on Sylvia.

"The letter doesn't say why, exactly, but I know there was some talk about expanding The Commons. I was under the impression that was some time in the future, but maybe that's why my name has moved up so quickly."

I don't think I like where this is going. I just had that long talk with Mark not two weeks back when he talked about Tiny and Nancy having that deadline staring them in the face and how he thought that was

why they went ahead and got married. I remember
thinking how glad I was that me and Molly could sort
of ease into the whole marriage thing, take it nice
and slow. I'm afraid Sylvia's going to put some
serious pressure on me to marry Molly so she won't
have to worry about her having a place to live or
somebody to take care of her.

"Do you know what this means, sweetie?"

I finally look over at Molly. She's looking at me
and has her hand back on Sylvia's arm.

"Maybe you'd better tell me," I say.

She turns to Sylvia. "Gram?"

Sylvia usually sips her wine, but this time she
takes a big drink and sets the glass down. She coughs
a little and wipes her eyes.

"Boone, when it comes time for me to move to The
Commons, we'd like," she looks at Molly, "I mean, I'd
like for you to move in here with Molly."

I'm glad I don't have a glass in my hand right
now, because I'm pretty sure I'd drop it.

"Unless, of course, you two have already, I
mean . . . ." Sylvia looks down at the letter and then
at Molly.

"Gram, you promised you wouldn't put any kind of
pressure on him about that," says Molly.

"I know, dear. It just slipped out.

"Now, when I get a firm date for my move I'll
decide when to put the house on the market, and I

don't know how long it will take for it to sell, and there would be a lot of decisions to be made about the house and the furniture and all my stuff, I mean what I can't take with me," and she looks like she's about to start crying.

She takes a deep breath and looks at me. "Do you remember a while back when you were going to have to move out of Ralph's place, and Molly suggested you move in here?"

I nod.

"If I remember correctly, you said you needed to have your own place, and very graciously declined her offer."

I nod again.

"Well, we were wondering if you'd be willing to reconsider that."

Damn, I did not see all this coming. I'm trying to think of what to say when Sylvia starts talking again.

"I would like for you to wait until I've moved out before you move in, that is, if you're willing to come live here. I know I'm being old-fashioned, but I think I would prefer to be settled in my new home before, well, before . . . ."

She puts down the letter and looks around. "I might like a refill, Molly dear, if you wouldn't mind."

"I'll get it, Gram."

"Thank you, dear. Now where did I put my glass?"

I stand up. "I think I've changed my mind about

not having a little wine." Molly is on her way to the kitchen and I follow her. As soon as we're in the kitchen I turn to her.

"Molly, what the hell?"

She's got her back to me. "It just came up after she got the letter. I mean, I never expected her to even be okay with me moving in with you, much less saying you can move in here."

I open the cabinet door and take a glass off the top shelf. "To tell you the truth, I hadn't even thought about Sylvia and The Commons, with the stuff with Momma and Frances, and then Tiny and Nancy laying that on us that night when I thought we were just going out to dinner.

"I got to tell you, I'm all mixed up about this. I mean, I love you more than anything and when I think about getting married someday you're the only one I see. That whole thing with Tiny just freaked me out something awful. When I talked to him it was like he felt like he was getting trapped or something. Not like I want to feel when it's time for me to get married."

"You want everything to be perfect, like it is in the movies?"

I don't answer her because I don't know exactly what she's talking about, since I haven't seen all that many movies and most of the ones I have seen have been full of car chases and gunfights.

Instead I pour the wine, and I'm about to pick up two of the glasses and head back into the sunroom when Molly says, "Hold on a second, Boone."

She's looking out at Sylvia. "I just want to make sure you understand how hard all this is for Gram. It's not just about you and me, or even about her moving into a new place. She's saying goodbye to a big part of her life. She knows that when she moves into The Commons she's never going to come back here."

All the places we lived when I was growing up I couldn't wait to get out of. Some of that was Daddy but some of it was the places weren't ours, and they weren't anything like as nice as this house is. I guess I get it that it's going to be hard for her, but whenever I've left a place I've been glad to get out of it. Except for Gamaliel's house. That was a good place to live. But it wasn't mine, and I wasn't there very long either. If Jerry hadn't been such an asshole about pretty much everything, it would have been a pretty good place to live for a while, but he just kept stirring shit up.

Anyway, I got nothing that even comes close to the way Sylvia has to feel about this place.

"And as far as you and me are concerned, you don't know Gram like I do. She's going against a lot of what she believes by asking you to move in here with me."

I don't say anything right off, just look at the glasses lined up on the counter. Picking up the one I just got out of the cabinet, I take a sip.

"I'm not trying to be hard on her, Molly. Like I said a minute ago, I'm all mixed up. Maybe I do want it to be like in the movies between you and me."

"I know you're not, and I've promised myself I'm not going to push you on this. I just want you to know how big a deal this is for her."

"I get it."

"Although," she says, and her voice changes. I look over at her and she's got a little smile on her face. "If you wait too long I may have to ask you myself."

First thing I think is how great that would be. All I'd have to do is say yes.

Next thing I think is, if you know you'd say yes why don't you just go ahead and ask her? All your talk to Tiny about him stepping up, and here you are just waiting for her to do all the work.

Molly says, "Hey, Boone, can you bring me my glass?"

I look around and she's gone. While I was standing there going round and round she had taken Sylvia's glass and headed back. I take her glass to her and say, "Sorry. Didn't realize you were gone."

"I could tell," she says. "Having to think over our offer?"

I shake my head. "You said about three months?"

Sylvia nods. "That's what the letter said. Of course, it could be more or less than that. It's not an exact date."

"Well, I was going to ask my landlord if I could do some work around the house, maybe fix it up a little bit, and have him take it off my rent. Maybe I'll hold off on that for now."

Sylvia takes a deep breath. "Okay. Okay."

I start to say something else and she holds up her hand. "It's all right, Boone, I know we kind of sprung this on you. You take as much time as you need to think about it. I'll take your decision not to talk to your landlord as a positive sign, and that's enough for me."

I nod, and look over at Molly. She's looking at me the way she hasn't in at least a couple of weeks, and I think, damn, I've missed that.

Chapter Twenty

Most of the landscaping kinds of jobs are falling off since we're getting into colder weather, so when Corey calls and asks me when I can come up to the warehouse I just pick a day in the middle of next week.

"That's actually perfect," he says. "Any chance you could bring Molly with you? I want to talk to you about some plans I've got and I've also made some changes I want her to try out."

When we get there Molly rolls up the new ramp and pushes the button under the sign that says, "Push to Enter." There's a little porch there, and she waits while the door slides sideways.

She turns to me. "He really goes all out, doesn't he?" She heads inside and the door starts to close behind her. I step up and nothing happens, so I go back and push the button.

Corey's waiting on the inside and I grin at him. "Thought you might have one of those automatic doors like at the grocery store."

He grins back. "I thought about it, but we're kind of out in the country here and I don't want a stray dog or a raccoon opening the door and wandering around."

Molly says, "I wondered why the button was behind that plastic shield. I had to slide my hand up underneath it to push the button."

"I figure that might make a difference. Those raccoons are smart, but they can't read."

I'm thinking raccoons are curious, too, and his idea will probably keep a dog out but it might not work for long against a raccoon.

"Anyway," he says, "if that doesn't work I'll just figure something else out. You like the changes I made?"

Molly nods. "It's great, Corey. Everything works just like it should."

"Good. Now, Boone, why don't we walk around in here and then a little bit outside the building, and I'll tell you about the next stage of this. Molly, you and Frankie are welcome to come along or have a look around if you'd rather."

He starts around the inside of the building talking about how the Museum of Appalachia is so big and how he wants to make this an intimate experience and something about "go deeper not wider" and I don't have any idea what he's talking about. It does

sound like he's going to want me to do some more
work for him so I try to act like I understand where
he's going with this, but it's hard. Molly and Frankie
stay with us for about halfway down the first aisle
and she gets interested in an old cabinet. Frankie
stays with her and it's just me and Corey.

"So I'm thinking along the lines of a retreat to a
simpler time," he says. We're outside now, behind the
building, and he points to the big field that his
warehouse is sitting on the edge of.

"I'd like to have a house here, just a small one,
that reflects the typical home in this area around the
first third of the twentieth century. That's the time
period the displays are concentrating on, and I'd like
to offer packages to folks who want to relive those
days, or show their families what it was like. Maybe
three days, a week at most." He's quiet for a minute
and then says, "I've got it in my head, but that's as
far as I've gone. Unless you're a general contractor,
I'll get someone to prep the site and build the house."
He looks over at me and I shake my head.

"It sounds real interesting, but I'm not the guy
you want to build a house from the ground up," I say,
even though I don't really mean the first part.
Actually it doesn't sound all that interesting, but I
figure he's not building this for people like me. People
like me, that couldn't wait to get out of that kind of
living, sure as hell wouldn't pay money to go back

and pretend we were doing it all over again.

Corey nods. "That's what I thought. I still want you in on this, Boone. You've been a good worker so far. I'm afraid I can't offer you any more than I've been doing already, a few days a couple of times a month. It's not going to be a steady job."

I wave my hand out over the field. "I'm fine with that, man. This thing you're talking about here is way more than I could do anyway, and I kind of like the arrangement we've got right now."

He grins and smacks me on the back. I've never liked that much, and I used to get all tensed up and ready to fight when it happened, but now it's just kind of irritating.

"Glad to hear that, Boone. I'm pretty satisfied with the way things are, too. So going into the winter I'll just call every now and then, but we'll pick up speed once spring hits and I can get the house started. It'll need furniture and all the stuff that goes into a place where people can live, not just walk through."

On the way back I tell Molly what Corey has in mind for the next stage of his big project, and she says, "Oh."

After a minute I say, "Is that all you've got to say about it?"

"Well, it's not like I'd ever be able to go there even if I wanted to, which I don't."

I look over at her, then back to the road.

"There wasn't any ADA back then, sweetie."

She's mentioned the ADA before. They're the part of the government that says businesses have to make sure that people like Molly can get into the buildings, go through doors, get to the second floor, and all the other stuff they couldn't do before because people didn't even think about them. Kind of like me before I met Molly.

"I bet Corey hasn't even thought about that."

She's looking over at Frankie. "Don't say anything, okay?"

"Why not?"

"Because he seems like a nice guy, and he knows me. I don't want him to have to decide between making it real and making it so I can use it if I want to."

"How the hell do you do that?"

"Do what?"

"Be so, you know, unselfish."

She laughs. "And here I thought you knew me. I can be pretty damned selfish sometimes."

The phone rings before I can say anything else, like tell her what she did for Nancy or this thing with Corey is pretty much the opposite of being selfish. It's wedged in between us and Molly pulls it out and says, "Hello." She gets a funny look on her face and says, "He's driving the truck right now. Hold on just a second." She covers the mouthpiece and whispers, "It's your mother."

It takes me a minute to think what to do. Finally I say, "We're just about eight or ten minutes from home. Tell her I'll call her back as soon as we get there."

I spend the next ten minutes trying to decide if I'm going to call her, and wondering what made her decide to call me now. I go round and round with that and can't come up with any kind of answer, so when we get home I shut off the engine and turn to Molly. "What do you think I need to do here?"

She puts her hand on my leg. "Let's get inside and you can call her back. I'll be right next to you, and I'll pinch you if you start to say something you can't take back. Like this," and she pinches my leg hard enough to make me flinch.

If I hadn't spent so much time with her I'd think she was serious, but I can see just a little bit of a smile around her eyes.

"Okay," I say, "but you better not pinch any harder than that or Momma'll think you're abusing me."

What I want to do is put this off as long as I can, but when Molly is sitting on the couch she pats the space next to her and says, "Come on, sweetie."

I sit down next to her and call Momma.

She answers on the first ring. "I was worried you

wouldn't call me back."

I can't think of what to say so I just say, "How are you, Momma?"

"I'm good, son, really good. I'm still in the same place, my job is great, and I, well, I've been thinking about calling Frances and I was just wondering if you think that's a good idea."

Molly can hear everything she's saying, and she squeezes my leg, not hard, and when I look over at her she nods.

"We were down to see her not all that long ago," I say. "She was in the hospital but she said she was going to be going back home real soon, so I bet she's back where she's living now."

"Oh, no! In the hospital? Is she all right? Why was she in a hospital?"

"You know, she never did say, exactly, but she seemed to be doing pretty good. I think she'd like it if you called her. She wrote a letter to you and gave it to me. It's already sealed and I can send it on to you if you want me to."

"What's in it?"

"I don't know, Momma. It's sealed up. I can send it on to you if you'll give me your address."

"Maybe I'll just ask her about it when I call. Say she's back at that home? I've got the number there."

"Probably. I mean, she talked like it'd be real soon that she was going back, and it's been a little while since we were there."

She doesn't say anything for what feels like a long time. Then she says, "So are you okay? That man, Mark, he says you're doing real well. How is it you know him again?"

I tell her about working at the home where I first saw Frances and how he's the preacher there.

"He sounds like a black man," she says.

"He is," I say.

"Well, you be careful, that's all I'm going to say about that."

"He's a good man, Momma. One of the best."

"Well . . . ." she says, and the way she says it is like every time anybody says something to her she doesn't like or disagrees with. She still won't stand up for herself. That "well . . . ." is the best she can do.

"So who was that answered your phone a little while ago?"

"That was Molly."

"She your girlfriend?"

I smile at Molly. "Yeah, Momma, she sure is."

We're both quiet this time, and I just wait for her to say something.

"Well, I hope she's a good girl." It's like she's trying to think of things to say to me.

"She is, Momma. She's the best thing that's ever happened to me."

"You sound like you might be asking her to get

married pretty soon."

I look at Molly again. She's red faced and trying to look everywhere except at me.

"I'm thinking pretty hard about it, Momma."

"Don't you do it, Boone Hammond," she says, and I'm surprised at how she sounds. "Don't you even think about it."

I don't say anything, and after a few seconds she goes on, "You know how things didn't work out between me and your daddy. You're better off on your own."

"I'm not like Daddy," I say.

She laughs, but it sounds angry. "I've seen him in you, Boone. You used to get so mad, and when I'd look at you I'd see Nate."

I'm afraid to look at Molly right now.

I've spent the last five or six years working as hard as I can to not be like Daddy. If you'd seen me right after she took off with Hannah, you'd probably agree with what she's saying, but I saw it too, and it scared the hell out of me.

I think Momma realizes she needs to get off the phone before we start arguing again. "I'm going to call Frances as soon as I hang up here. I feel bad about the way we left it the last time. Why don't you hang onto that letter for a little bit, at least until I've had a chance to talk to her. I'll call you back and give you my address."

"Okay, Momma. You take care, now."

"You too, son," and she's gone.

I sit there on the couch for as long as I can stand it and start to get up. Molly puts her hand on my leg again and says, "Stay here with me for just a minute, sweetie. Please?"

"Okay."

She takes a deep breath. "Was that as hard on you as it was on me?"

"Why did she have to say that about me?" I'm pretty close to crying, or cussing, or throwing the phone across the room. But I don't do any of those things.

"You're not like him, sweetie. You hear me?"

I want to believe her, but I also want to tell her she never met him so she doesn't really know what she's talking about.

"The last time she had anything to do with me I probably was on my way to being just like him. You didn't know me then, Molly. I was awful mad at just about everything."

She takes hold of my chin and turns my head to face her. "I know you now. I know what kind of man you are. That kid she was talking about, she might know him, but she doesn't know you. Not like I do."

"I'm still pretty pissed off that she'd say that kind of thing. She didn't used to be mean like that."

Molly says, "I don't know what to tell you about

that, sweetie. From what you've told me, she's just getting out from under a pretty bad situation."

"It was bad, for sure."

After a minute she says, "I was thinking about what you told her about me."

"Listen, I know I was kind of stumbling all over myself there. I just didn't know she was going to do that whole thing about you being a good girl and all. I almost said, you mean woman, but I figured she wouldn't get it."

Molly laughs out loud. "Probably she wouldn't."

"You know I've told you before, you're the best thing that's ever happened to me."

"It's mutual, sweetie."

She leans her head back and stares up at the ceiling. "What time is it?"

I look at my phone. "About three. We got to Corey's place late morning, and . . . damn, we never got any lunch."

"That's okay. Gram will have something for us later on. I was just thinking, we've got time for an afternoon nap before we go over to the house."

I look at her. "A nap? I got to tell you, I'm not really all that tired."

"Me neither," she says, and she's got a little smile on her face when she tilts her head toward the bedroom. "Come on, sweetie. Let's get in there while we've still got some time."

Chapter Twenty-One

"You know, Frankie, I'm glad you're not the jealous type," says Molly, scratching her behind one ear. We're about half way to Sylvia's and up until now we've both been just riding along. We know how to be together without having to talk all the time, and I've just mainly been feeling really good.

"The only reason she left us alone was because I closed the door," I say.

"Is that true, Frankie?" She gives her one more scratch and turns to me. "Feeling better, sweetie?"

I give her a look. "There's no way I could ever feel better than I do right now."

"That's the right answer," she says and laughs.

We tell Sylvia all about Corey's new plans and the first thing she says is, "Oh, I'd love to go to a place like that!" She turns to Molly. "Next summer, after I'm settled in at The Commons, you and Boone can come and get me and we'll spend a few nights there."

Then it hits her and she says, "He's going to make

it so you can go, isn't he?"

"Boone and I talked about that on the way to his place," Molly says. "If he makes it real, I won't be able to enjoy myself at all. I can't imagine he's going to put everything on one level and install ramps instead of steps, or make the doorways wide enough for a wheelchair."

"But he needs to make it accessible," Sylvia says.

Molly shakes her head. "I've been thinking about this, Gram. If he makes it just like it was a hundred years ago, then any family that has somebody like me in it will have to deal with the way it used to be. Might be a good reminder for whoever visits his, his . . . . " She turns to me. "Do you know what he's going to call this thing?"

I shake my head. "No idea. I got to say, Sylvia, I thought the same thing when Molly reminded me of how it used to be, and I was all ready to tell Corey he needed to make all the accommodations. Now that I think about it, though, Molly's right. It can either be real or it can be fixed up for her. Can't be both."

Sylvia doesn't like it, I can tell, but she doesn't say anything else about it. We help her get the food out of the kitchen and on the table, and we sit down to eat.

Molly tells her about answering the phone while I was driving and it being Momma, and Sylvia says, "Well, how did that go? Does she know about you and Boone?"

Molly and I look at each other. "Could have been better," I say, and she nods.

I don't tell her everything Momma said, because some of it was just meanness and I don't feel right spreading that around.

"She did say she hoped Molly was a good girl," I say.

Sylvia smiles. "And what did you tell her?"

"I told her Molly's the best thing that's ever happened to me."

Sylvia nods. "I hope that satisfied her."

"Well, Momma and I are trying to figure stuff out right now," I say, because I don't know how much I want to tell Sylvia about what Momma's like now.

Pretty much the whole time she and Daddy were together, especially after Frankie died, I kept waiting for her to push back, stand up for herself, say something back to him, and she never did. I guess now she's standing up some, and I don't like it much. Something else to talk to Mark about next time I'm down there.

I don't know what I would've done if Mark hadn't stuck with me. The first time I met him was at Gamaliel's funeral, and he had me up there telling stories about the old man before I knew it. I was so pissed off at him I threatened to kick his ass, and when he said he guessed he'd have to take it because he'd do it again, I couldn't help but like the guy. He's been a good friend, and I sure need to talk to him about this.

"Sweetie, you still with us?" Molly is tapping on the back of my hand.

"Yeah, I'm here."

"Boone, you were a thousand miles away just then," says Sylvia. "Are you sure everything's all right?"

I nod. "I was just thinking it might be a good idea if I went down to see Mark pretty soon."

"That is a very good idea," says Molly. "You can give him a call after we finish eating. Right now I need some more of those mashed potatoes."

I pass them to her and try to get back to eating. Sylvia cooks the way a lot of people around here do, so it's mostly food I grew up on, and she's a good cook. She eats fish a lot of the time, which we never did, but I can eat pretty much anything that's fried. Tonight it's mashed potatoes, fried okra, and some kind of fish we've had before. She calls it tilapia, and I don't know exactly what that is, but she puts some kind of seasoning on it and fries it up good and crisp. It's a good meal.

"This is great, Sylvia," I say.

She bows her head a little. "Thanks, Boone. It's been a while since I made pineapple upside-down cake, but as soon as the oven dings we can pull it out and let it start cooling."

"I hope you've got vanilla ice cream," says Molly.

I try Mark at the home after the pineapple upside-down cake, but there's no answer at his office, and the person who covers the phones there says he left about 5:30.

Sylvia is making coffee. "You'll catch him tomorrow, I'm sure. Would you like a drop of brandy in your coffee, Boone?"

We sit and talk about nothing in particular until Sylvia says, "I've been walking through this old place a lot lately. I think I'm going to get in touch with T he Commons and find out how much room I'll have up there. I have to tell you, even though there's a lot of things here I will hate to part with, there's even more junk." She laughs. "I hadn't really given it much thought until now, but we added a lot more than we subtracted over the years. Once I got over the initial shock of thinking about leaving this place, I realized that quite a bit of what is here I'm not really attached to. I suppose everybody does it, but I feel like I've been a bit lazy."

I can't help it. I start laughing, and by the time I get myself under control they're both staring at me like I've lost my mind.

"Sylvia," I say when I can talk again, "you have no idea how much junk some people have in their houses. This," I wave my hand around, "is nothing compared to some of the places I've seen. There was this one house, I could barely get through it. And some of the sheds and barns, I mean, it took me a half a day to clear away enough brush to get the truck up to one shed I was working on last month, and when I opened the door I couldn't even step inside."

"I suppose maybe it's not as bad as it could be," she says. "Still, there's a lot."

"There always is," I say, "at least that's what I've seen. You've got some time to figure out which is the really good stuff."

When I try Mark the next day I get him on the first try. I barely get to say 'hi' before he says, "Have you talked to your mother lately?"

When I don't answer right away he says, "I'm going to assume you have, and that's why you're calling. I spoke to her myself not too many days ago."

"I know," I say, "and that's part of why I'm calling you. You got any time in the next few days we can come down and see you?"

"Sure, let me look." I hear some papers rustling, and he's back. "Day after tomorrow is the soonest I can really give you more than a few minutes. Is that too far away?"

I shake my head. "No, that's good. What time should we come down?"

He says middle of the morning, and I say, "I'll tell Molly and we'll see you then. One thing before I let you go, man. Momma asked me if I was thinking about asking Molly to marry me.”

“Seems like a reasonable question to me.”

“Well, yeah, but Molly was sitting right there listening to us talk in case me and Momma started getting into it.”

He laughs. “I guess that could be a little awkward.”

“It was pretty bad. I said I was thinking real hard about it, and she said, ‘Don’t you do it, Boone Hammond.’ Just like that, real mad like.”

He’s quiet for a second. “Molly heard that part too?”

“Yeah. We talked about it some after the call. I’ll tell you about it when we see you.”

When we get to the home we’re not even out of the parking lot before Betty comes running up to us.

“Did you hear about Tiny and Nancy? They’re getting married! It’s going to be up in the Smokies with all the fall colors, week after next, and you know Nancy’s mother is just over the moon!”

I don’t look down at Molly, I just say, “Tiny told me a while ago he was thinking about it.”

“We saw them the night he proposed,” Molly says. “Nancy was so happy, she was just in tears.”

Betty looks kind of disappointed that we already knew about Tiny and Nancy, but before she can say anything else I say, “We were on our way in to see

Mark. Is he here yet?"

She says, "The last time I saw him he was in the hallway."

"Thanks," I say.

"Are you going to the wedding?" asks Molly.

"Well, of course!" Betty says. "Old friend of the family, you know."

The first thing Mark says when we get into his office is, "Did Betty catch you in the parking lot or wait until you were all the way inside the building?"

Molly laughs. "She let us get out of the truck, but that was about it."

"I don't think she knows why they're in such a hurry, but she might suspect."

Molly looks at me and I say, "He kind of tricked me into that part but, yeah, he knows."

"Don't worry, Molly," Mark says. "I'm good at keeping things in confidence." He looks at me. "Have you two been invited to the wedding?"

I shake my head. "I'd be real surprised if Stan would let me anywhere near the church, or wherever they're going to have it."

"Nancy told me he still blames you for her taking off like she did," says Molly. "The way it's turned out, maybe he ought to thank you. I think that might have been the beginning of Tiny and Nancy getting together."

I kind of wish she hadn't reminded me of that. It

took me a while to get over being really pissed at both of them for lying to me about them not being together and how worried about me they were and all that shit, when they were probably already doing it. Of course me and Tiny, we didn't take all that long to get back to being good with each other. It took a lot longer with Nancy, and the only reason I got over it at all with either one of them was because I met Molly.

That makes me think maybe I ought to thank Nancy for taking off on me like that and Tiny for moving in on me. It got me together with Molly, and I can't even imagine not being with her.

I laugh out loud when I think about doing that, and Molly and Mark look at me like I'm crazy.

"Are you okay, sweetie?"

I nod. It takes me a second to stop laughing enough to tell them why I kind of lost it. By the time I finish explaining they're laughing too.

"Maybe I'll sneak into the reception and do one of those toasts, you know, like Raymond does all the time." Molly nods, and I go on in a big voice. "I'd like to thank Nancy for running out on me and and Tiny for moving in on me. It sent me straight to the best girl — I mean woman — in the world."

Mark's got a big grin on his face, but he's shaking his head. "Don't you dare, Boone."

"I know, man. I wouldn't have the balls to do that

even if I thought I could."

He stands up. "You two want anything from the cafeteria? Coffee?"

Molly raises her hand. "Coffee would be nice. A little cream, please."

"Make mine black," I say.

He's back in just a couple of minutes. This time of day the cafeteria's pretty much empty.

Frankie settles in next to Molly and I sit down. Mark leans back in his chair and says, "So you talked to your mother?"

"Yeah, Molly answered the phone while I was driving, so I called her back after we got home." I take a breath and Molly puts her hand on my arm. "It was hard, Mark. It was like we were trying to make each other understand stuff and not getting anywhere."

He waits. Mark is real good at that, just waiting.

"I mean, it started out okay. She was talking about Frances and wanting to call her, but when she asked about you it started getting weird."

"She asked about me?"

"Well, she wanted to know if you were black, and when I said yes she said I should be careful. Then she asked about Molly and, well, I told you part of that day before yesterday. It's like she thinks I'm still this kid, the one she just left there to deal with Daddy, and I'm wondering if she thought I was turning out like him and she needed to get away from both of us at the same time."

When I stop talking Molly jumps in. "It's like she's not giving Boone any credit for growing up over the last five or six years."

Mark sets his cup down and leans forward. "As far as Natalie is concerned, Boone, you still are that kid. That's the only Boone she knows."

While he's talking I'm thinking about what I said to Momma, about Molly being the best thing that ever happened to me. It's true, and I can't even think about not being with her, and I don't really give a damn about what Tiny and Nancy are doing or whether it looks like I'm trying to copy him or anything else.

I realize it's quiet in the room, and Molly and Mark are both looking at me. Mark says, "Are you okay, Boone?"

I nod. "Yeah, I'm good." I turn to Molly. "I don't know how this kind of thing is supposed to work, and I know this isn't some kind of fancy place," and I see her lip start to tremble a little, "and if I tried to do something like that I'd probably screw it up anyway. I'm not smart enough to figure out the perfect time or place or anything else, and I'm tired of going round and round in my head about it." I'm scared as hell, but I've said so much already I figure it's too late to stop now.

"I think we ought to get married, if you'll have me. There's nobody I'd rather be with than you, and when I try to think about not being with you it doesn't even make any sense at all. I promise I'll get you a ring real soon if you say yes, and we can take our time and not be in a hurry like Tiny and Nancy are, and —"

"Sweetie, if you want me to say yes you're going to have to stop talking and let me get a word in." Molly is laughing and crying at the same time, and Mark's got a huge grin on his face.

"I was prepared to spend some time with you helping you plan how to propose to this lovely woman, but I guess you don't need that now," he says. "I do insist on being the one to perform the ceremony. I wouldn't miss this one for the world."

Chapter Twenty-Two

"So do we tell Sylvia right now, or wait?"

We're on our way back from Mark's office, and neither one of us can stop smiling. I'm so glad to get that behind me I don't know what to do, and Molly is still wiping away tears every now and then.

"No, not right now," she says. "I'd rather wait until I have a ring, see how long it takes her to notice it."

It's as hard to keep a good secret as it is to keep a bad one. I didn't figure on that happening, but it sure is hard to pretend around Sylvia. I bet Molly has it a lot worse, but it was her idea.

I'm spending a lot of time thinking about how to pick out a ring and coming up empty. I don't know anything about how to do this, and it's making me crazy. I think about asking Tiny what he did, but I saw the ring he got for Nancy and I know there's no way in hell I can afford something like that. I don't think about calling Momma or Aunt Claire to ask about what kind of ring I'm supposed to get, but I do think about Frances.

I've been at this for a week or more when I get a call from Corey.

"Hey Boone, if you're not too covered up I need you for a day, two at the most. I'm trying to get the inside exhibits into some kind of shape and I'll be moving stuff around."

I tell him tomorrow works for me, and he says to come up around 9:00 and we'll get going.

He's got a plan for how he wants the different areas laid out and it turns out we have to swap around three of them. Everything that's in all three of them has to come out, all at the same time, and then they have to be put back together in a different place. I don't see the point in it myself, but he's got it in his head, and it's a little money coming in.

When we stop for lunch the first day I tell him about me and Molly. He's all excited for me, tells me what a lucky guy I am and all that stuff.

"Problem is, I don't know anything about getting her a ring," I say. "I just sort of asked her out of the blue and didn't even think about having a ring before I did, so now I'm trying to figure out what to get her."

He doesn't answer me and when I look over at him he's got this big grin on his face and he says, "Just wait right here," and he goes around to the other side of the warehouse. When he comes back he's got one of those brown envelopes in his hand, the ones with the little metal things on the flap end that let you close it up without licking it, and hands it to me.

I take it from him and look at it. It's kind of dusty, and about half the size of a regular white envelope.

"Open it," he says.

I bend the metal tabs up and open the flap. When I tilt it, a ring slides out and lands in the palm of my hand.

"I found it last week in one of the old cabinets I've had here almost since the beginning. No idea where it came from, so I can't return it. That the kind of thing you're looking for?"

It's kind of dirty, but it looks like it's probably a nice ring. There's a little stone, and the ring has some kind of pattern carved into it.

"It's real nice," I say. I don't know if it's the right kind of ring or not, but it looks good, or would if it was cleaned up. "What do you want for it?"

"How about two days' work?"

I don't know whether he's kidding or not. I'm still not real good at figuring that kind of thing out, and I don't know what to say.

I finally say, "You sure?"

He shrugs. "I was going to have it appraised and get it cleaned up, but I'm not sure how I'd display it if I kept it for the warehouse. Your Molly seems like a real nice lady. I bet she'd like to have a ring as soon as you could get her one, and all you'd need to do with this one is get it cleaned up and sized for her."

"You sure?" I know I'm repeating myself, but I can't think of anything else to say.

He laughs. "You understand, I'm planning to work your ass off for the next day and a half. So yeah, I'm sure."

I take the ring to Mark and tell him what happened. He looks at it and says, "Let me see if I can get this cleaned up for you and I'll have a guy I know take a look at it."

When I go back a couple of days later Mark says, "I had my friend clean it up and give me his opinion of the ring." He opens the middle drawer of his desk and takes out a clear plastic bag with the ring in it. He hands it to me.

"It cleans up real nice, I think." I'm looking at it and I got to say it doesn't look like the same ring. "My friend thinks it's old, based on the design, but not antique. He thinks mid twentieth century.

"It's in very good condition, aside from the dirt and dust. As far as the value of the ring, he says it's no Hope Diamond."

I don't have any idea what that is, and I guess Mark can tell.

"The Hope is a famous diamond, very rare and valuable. This ring is, as I said, in good condition, and is probably worth a few hundred dollars. I think it is going to look great on Molly's finger."

"What if it doesn't fit?"

"It probably won't. Usually rings have to be sized. You'll go to a jeweler and they'll measure her finger. You leave the ring with them and they call you when it's ready."

I'm starting to get scared. What if Momma's right and I'm just like Daddy? I'm about to get married, and I remember what it was like being in that house when I was a kid. It was awful. I don't want to put Molly or anybody else through that.

When I realize Mark's been talking the whole time I've been just sitting here staring at the ring, I start listening again. " . . . and maybe after you finish at the jeweler's, you two can go out to eat somewhere nice."

He notices the look on my face, I guess, because he stops and says, "What's wrong?"

I tell him what I'm worrying about and he leans back in his chair. "I can see that."

"What the hell?" I can't believe he's saying that I might treat Molly the way Daddy treated Momma. "You're agreeing with Momma?"

He shakes his head. "No, but I can see your mother saying something like that, since the last time she saw you was five or six years ago. She has no idea how you've turned things around, Boone."

"Molly said pretty much the same thing."

He smiles. "I am not surprised. It does bring up an interesting question, though."

"What's that?"

"Are you going to invite her to the wedding? It's customary, and she is family, after all."

I sit back in the chair and stare up at the ceiling. I hadn't really thought about inviting any of my friends or family to the wedding, and the first thing that comes to me sounds like something that might blow the whole thing up.

"Oh, shit. If we're talking about inviting family, that means Momma and Hannah and Aunt Claire and Frances might all be in the same room at the same time."

"Yes, it would."

"You going to hire security for this, Mark?"

He laughs, but I'm only about half kidding. If Momma and Aunt Claire got into it, and they might if Hannah's right there to remind them of why they're mad at each other, it could be bad.

If it was up to me, I'd have Tiny and Nancy there, and Raymond and Charlotte, and Joaquin and P. J. from Memphis, and Corey and whoever. I don't really know much about him, so I don't know if he's got a wife or a girlfriend or what. Not sure I'd want anybody else, at least from my side of things.

"Don't guess there's any chance we could just sneak in here one morning and have you do your thing, be done with it."

Mark shakes his head. "I'm pretty sure Molly is going to want a little more pomp and circumstance than that."

I don't even know what that is either. Like the Hope Diamond. Mark's throwing all kinds of shit at me that I don't know anything about.

"What are you talking about?"

"I think Molly's looking forward to a chance to celebrate more than just doing what you have to do to be officially married." He grins. "I think she wants to show you off a little bit."

"I guess I could give Momma and Hannah the letters Frances wrote them an hour or so ahead of time. Maybe that would keep them busy."

I don't even want to think about all this stuff. I don't know anything about planning a wedding, and I'm not sure I want to know. Maybe Molly and Sylvia can take care of all this.

"Actually, Boone, the wedding planning is the responsibility of the bride's family," Mark says. I swear, sometimes I think this guy is a mind reader. "My experience at being in on more than a few weddings is that your job is to stay out of the way and show up on the right day at the right time."

I can do that. Hell, anybody can do that.

"Okay," I say. "You pretty sure about that?"

I get a couple of ideas from Mark about places to

go to get the ring sized, and when I get home I call Molly.

"You know that place down on Market Square you told me you wanted to try?"

"Tupelo Honey?"

"You want to go down there tomorrow and see if it's any good?"

She gives me a funny look the next day when I head toward my place instead of Knoxville. I make up some lame excuse about having to stop by the house for something. I can tell she's not buying it, but she goes along.

When we get inside I help her onto the couch and say, "Okay, I lied about having to come by here and check on something."

"I know. You're a lousy liar, sweetie."

I pull the ring out of my pocket. "I figure if you don't like it I'd rather hear about it in private. If you do, there's a jewelry store on the way where we can stop and drop it off to be sized."

She just sits there for a long time, and I start to think maybe she really doesn't like it. Then she holds out her hand and says, "Let's see what it looks like when it's where it belongs."

I start to slide it on and she says, "The other finger," and wiggles her ring finger at me. I slide it on and it fits like it was made just for her.

"Oh," she says. "Oh, my."

She stretches her arm out and turns her hand one way and another. I got to say it looks good, at least I think it does.

She's still staring at the ring. "Where did you get this? It's so beautiful!"

I think about telling her I bought it at a fancy jewelry store, but end up telling her about Corey offering it to me instead of paying me in cash for the last few days of work I did for him.

"He just happened to have this laying around?"

"Well, it didn't look like that when I got it. Mark took it to a friend of his to have it cleaned and get an idea of what kind of ring it is. He says it's no Hope Diamond."

She laughs out loud. "No, and I'm glad it's not. That would be too ostentatious. This is perfect. Perfect."

Ostentatious. Another word I don't know. I'm sure getting a lot of that right now. It doesn't matter, though. She said it was perfect.

"You sure it's okay?"

"Oh, sweetie, it's so much better than okay."

I call the restaurant and make a reservation. When we get there we still have fifteen minutes or so, which is just about enough for one trip around the Square. It's a nice place, different every time I come down here. There's a sign saying it won't be long until they put up the skating rink, and at first I think they're talking about roller skating.

"Why do they need something special just for skating?"

Some guy standing next to us hears me and says, "Ice skating, dude." He says something to the girl with him and they're laughing as they walk away.

I'm thinking about going after them when Molly says, "It's about time for our table, sweetie." She puts her hand on my arm. "Let's go show off my ring to the waiter."

We turn around and head back. We've only gone a few steps when she looks up at me and says, "That's how I know your mother is wrong about you being just like your father. From what you've told me, he would never have had the self-control to walk away from that."

I don't say anything, but she's right. If Daddy had thought that guy was laughing at him he'd have gone after him in a heartbeat. Hell, five years ago I'd have done it too, which I guess is why Momma thinks I'm just like him. Maybe Mark and Molly are right about Momma just being a few years behind, judging me on what I used to be. I wonder if she'll ever get to know me the way I am now. Probably not, her being so far away.

"So," she says, "ever been ice skating?"

"No."

"I went a few times before my accident. Never got

past being pretty terrible at it." She's quiet for a second. "Guess that's as good as I'll ever be."

I don't know what to do when she talks about this kind of thing. Nothing I can think of seems like a good thing to say, so I just keep walking beside her.

Chapter Twenty-Three

The restaurant says it's Southern cooking, and I guess it is, but we never had anything this fancy at our house when I was growing up. Even though it isn't the kind of stuff I'm used to, it's real good. We take our time eating and split the banana pudding for dessert.

"When the weather gets warmer we'll go over to the ice cream shop on Gay Street," Molly says. "I hear good things about it."

We get back to Sylvia's kind of late, but she's still up, and I swear it takes her about three seconds to notice the ring.

"Come over here, dear," says Sylvia. "Let me have a good look at it."

"Well, that took about as long as I thought it would," Molly whispers to me.

She rolls over to Sylvia and stretches out her hand. Sylvia leans forward and stares at the ring, and her hand trembles a little when she takes Molly's and turns it to get a better look.

They're both staring at it and getting all teary-eyed, and I say, "I better get back home. I don't usually leave Frankie alone this long."

"You go get that beautiful girl and drive right back over here," says Sylvia. "And bring one of your good bottles of wine when you come. We'll have a celebration!"

When we get back Sylvia's in the kitchen. I look at Molly and she shrugs. "I told her we'd already eaten, but she just waved me off. I have no idea what she's up to in there."

Frankie says hi to Bert and Ray and settles into her spot, and I sit down next to Molly. She reaches for my hand and squeezes it. "I've never seen her this happy, not since I moved in with her. She's on cloud nine."

I point to the wine on the table. "I didn't know what y'all would want, so I brought two. A bottle of red and a bottle of white."

"It all depends upon your appetite," Molly whispers, smiling.

I look at her and she says, "Never mind, sweetie. Reminded me of an old song. Let's see if Gram will tell us which one to open."

We're about to get up when Sylvia comes out of the kitchen carrying a tray. "If I'd known we were going to be celebrating, I'd have been prepared," she says, and gives Molly a look. "All I have is a little plate of finger foods, cheese and vegetables and crackers, and a couple of different kinds of dip if you want that. It's not much, I'm afraid."

She sets the tray down and looks at it. "I'm almost ashamed to open one of these fancy bottles of wine when this is all we have."

"It's fine, Sylvia," I say. "I know we kind of sprung this on you. It looks real good, and all I need to know is whether you're supposed to drink red wine or white wine with it."

"Oh!" she says. "I hope I can find that old corkscrew I used to have."

Sylvia and Molly both think I should open the white wine, so after we find a corkscrew I get three glasses and pour a half glass for all of us. Sylvia goes to the kitchen and opens the freezer door. "Anybody else want an ice cube?"

I know Raymond wouldn't even think about drinking white wine without it being chilled to the right temperature, but we're kind of making this up as we go along, so me and Molly both say yes.

It's been long enough since we ate that I'm kind of hungry, so I go for the cheese and crackers. Molly and Sylvia like vegetables, so it all works out, and we sit around eating and drinking and smiling at each other until the wine and food are all gone.

I stand up and poke Frankie with my toe. "Up and

at 'em, girl. It's way late and we need to get on out of here."

Molly looks at Sylvia. She gets this funny look on her face and takes a couple of deep breaths, then shakes her head. "I'm sorry, dear, I just can't do it. I'm so sorry."

"It's okay, Gram," Molly says.

She turns to me. "I'll see you to the door."

When we get to the door I say, "What was that all about?"

"That was about Gram not being able to say you could spend the night here," Molly says.

"Oh," I say. "Well, I guess I get that."

"Me, too," says Molly. "Now I better get back in there and try to keep her from feeling bad about it. It's really okay, right? I mean, with both of us?"

"It's okay."

I look over at Frankie, sitting at her normal spot with her nose up against the window where I've got it cracked open. "Won't be long until it's too cold to do that, girl."

She doesn't even turn her head.

The next couple of weeks go by pretty quick. I get a call from Tiny apologizing all over himself for not inviting me to the wedding. I get it, and that's what I tell him. There's no way Stan would let me anywhere near that church or wherever they're doing the ceremony, and I'm pretty sure I don't want to see him either.

I think Nancy feels even worse about not inviting Molly, especially since Molly was so good to her when she didn't even have to be. Molly's cool with not going. She knows enough about my history with Stan to know I can't be there, and she doesn't want to be there without me.

We haven't told anybody yet about us getting engaged, but I'm thinking about calling Raymond and Charlotte.

When I get Raymond on the phone the first thing he says is, "Well, Boone, have you decided to do the smartest thing you could possibly do and ask young Molly to be your bride?"

"Well, as a matter of fact, that's why I'm calling," I say, and there's a long silence.

"Charlotte!" I hear him calling. "Would you come here, please? I have Boone on the phone."

It takes her a minute to get there and I'm just grinning into the phone. I look over at Molly, sitting next to me on the couch, and she is too.

"Okay, Boone, Charlotte is here. Would you repeat for her what you just shared with me?"

When I tell her Charlotte claps her hands. "That is such wonderful news! Please tell Molly how very happy we are for her."

"She's right here, Charlotte. You can tell her yourself."

We go back and forth with them for a while and they are so happy a couple of times Raymond forgets to sound like he's making some kind of speech.

We promise to tell them when we've set a date and when we finally get off the phone Molly says, "They are such nice people."

It goes great when we call Frances, and Hannah, and about as good as I figured it would when we call Momma. She says she's glad for us and then says she's got to go and gets off the phone.

"Okay," I say. "That about does it for me. You want to tell Nancy and let her tell Tiny, or you want me to call Tiny?"

"I'll call Nancy. I've been wanting to talk to her anyway."

"Well, that leaves your family."

She's quiet for a long time. "Gram already knows, sweetie."

"I, I was thinking about your parents."

Molly hasn't said hardly anything about her mom and dad since I've gotten to know her. When she talks about family it's always Sylvia.

"You know my parents split up," she says. "It wasn't a friendly divorce, and I haven't heard from Dad since right after it happened. I think he's married and living on the West Coast, but I'm not even sure.

"Mom, well, she hasn't really dealt with this," and

she pats the armrest of her wheelchair. "She gets real uncomfortable even talking on the phone. It's like she doesn't know how to talk to me or what to say, so we don't talk. I haven't seen her in a while either. If you're wondering who's going to walk me down the aisle, it'll be Gram. She's the only one it could be."

I feel like a damned fool for not noticing this before now. She's always been right beside me while I deal with my family's shit, and I never asked about hers. Too wrapped up in my own stuff to even see that Sylvia is the only family she ever talks about.

I'm almost afraid to ask the next question, because I figure I know the answer already.

"So, you got some friends you want to invite?"

She looks down at her hands resting in her lap. "I was kind of hoping you'd let me share yours, you know, Raymond and Charlotte, Tiny and Nancy. I really don't, I mean, that'd be okay, right?"

She raises her head and says, "I'd rather not talk about guest lists and stuff like that right now. I mean, we don't even know when this is going to happen."

She looks so sad I figure I'd better find something else to talk about, so I tell her about the job I'm working on now. It's pretty boring, the same kind of thing I've done a dozen times already. A guy that lives about a half hour away needs a winter shelter for some goats he bought back in the spring, I'm cleaning out the little barn he was using as a storage shed.

She tries to act like she's interested, but in just a few minutes she says, "It's been a long day, sweetie, and I'm pretty tired. Maybe you could just take me home?"

"It's kind of early. Why don't you stick around for a while?"

All of a sudden, she's mad at me. "I guess I forgot to say please. Would you please take me home now?"

I can feel myself getting mad right back.

"Sure. Let's go."

Neither one of us says a word all the way back to Sylvia's and when we get to the door she doesn't invite me in and I don't ask.

"See you tomorrow," I say.

"I guess," she says, and I turn around and leave.

First time in a long time we didn't kiss goodnight.

All the way home I'm thinking, what the hell just happened? I thought things were going great, and we'd talked to a bunch of people that were real happy about us getting married, and then it all went straight to hell.

I had left Frankie at home because I figured I wouldn't be staying, and when I get home and open the door she looks past me like, "Where's Molly?"

"She's at Sylvia's, girl, and I don't know when I'm going to see her again. She's really pissed about

238

something."

We don't talk at all the next day. I feel real bad about that but I don't know if I'm supposed to call her or wait on her to call me.

"If I don't hear from her tomorrow, I'm either calling her or going over there," I tell Frankie.

She just looks out the window. We're driving back from the job I was telling Molly about, and it's done except for about an hour and a half tomorrow morning to finish cleaning up. After that I've got a solid week with nothing on the calendar. I kind of knew it was going to slow down, so I'm not worried about it, but I don't want to just sit at home either. I think about going to see Hannah, but I don't want to go without Molly. Hannah will have a thousand questions if I show up with just Frankie, and besides, that other kid's still there, the one that freaked out as soon as she saw Frankie. I can't leave her here all day, so I guess I'm not going to see my little sister this week.

I finish the job the next morning, the guy pays me, and I'm about to pull out on the road when my phone rings.

Chapter Twenty-Four

It's not a number I recognize, and I'm kind of disappointed that it's not Molly, but I figure it's maybe another job, so I answer it.

"Hello."

"I'm looking for Boone Hammond."

"You got him."

He doesn't say anything.

"Something I can do for you?"

Still nothing, and I'm about to hang up when he does.

"That was weird," I tell Frankie. "Wonder what he wanted."

We swing by the bank and put about half the money in my account. Most of the people I work for, including this guy, pay in cash. I guess I ought to keep better records of how much is coming in, but I haven't got started doing that yet.

That makes me think of that time up at Raymond's he started talking about when Molly was going to start helping with the business, and that makes me think I ought to call her. Just get it over with, instead of waiting for her to do something. I figure the worst thing she can do is hang up on me.

When we get home I clean out the truck, make sure Frankie has fresh water, and sit down on the couch. I take out the phone and sit there staring at it for a minute. I'm not sure what I'm going to say, and I don't much like feeling like that either.

I'm about to call her anyway when the phone rings again. Same number as before. I answer it and say, "If you got something to say to me, go ahead and say it."

He doesn't answer and I'm about to hang up on him when he says, "Hey, Boone, it's Curt."

It's been five years since I've talked to him, but once he says who he is I recognize the voice.

"It's been a while."

"It has, man. How're you doing?"

"I'm good." I guess I'm supposed to ask about him, but the last I remember him he was hanging out with that bunch of guys who were Mr. Timmons' gang at school, making fun of me right along with the rest of them.

"That's good," he says. "That's good."

I really can't think of anything to say to this guy. I mean, he was a friend of mine, but it was a long time ago. I guess he was a friend.

"Did you need something, Curt?"

"Well, yeah, there is something," he says.

After a minute he says, "I need some help with a job I've got coming up, and I thought about you."

This doesn't make any sense at all. I don't even know how he tracked me down.

"How did you get my number, Curt? I mean, it's been years since you wanted to have anything to do with me. Last I remember, you were running with Timmons' gang."

He doesn't answer, and right then it hits me. Timmons went to jail, and so did a bunch of the students that were following him around, and Curt was the guy who spilled his guts to the police to keep himself out of trouble. I never would have figured Curt for a criminal, but I really didn't know him after he dumped me for Timmons' boys. Who knows what all they were into. Who knows what he's into now.

"So what kind of a job is this exactly? Cause I'm thinking it might not be anything I want any part of."

He hangs up right then.

I put the phone down and look over at Frankie. "Damn, girl, that was, well, I don't know what all that was."

What I'm thinking is if I hadn't met Nancy and Tiny, I might be right in the middle of whatever Curt is doing. Hell, I might be in jail along with whichever of Curt's friends he gave up to the police.

I call Tiny. He answers after about four rings.

"Hey, Boone. I was going to call you."

"Did you give Curt my number?"

"Who's Curt?"

Tiny was a couple of grades ahead of us in school, so I guess it makes sense he doesn't know the name.

"Guy I knew in high school. Got mixed up in that whole Timmons thing. He just called me, out of the blue, and I haven't seen him in five years or more. I'm trying to figure out how he tracked me down."

I hear him say, "It's Boone, babe," and when he comes back on he says, "Nancy wants to talk to Molly when we're done."

"Molly's over at Sylvia's. It's just me and Frankie here right now."

"Okay," he says. "I'll let her know. She can get her over there.

"I don't know anybody named Curt, but it's not like I've been keeping your number a secret or anything. Seems like Nick asked me a week or so ago if I was still in touch with you, and I think your name has come up once or twice since you were at my place for that cookout. You did make kind of an impression, you know. I don't remember anybody acting like they needed you right away or anything like that. Why, what was Curt wanting?"

"Wanted me to help him with some job. It sounded kind of off and he was, you know, nervous on the phone and all. When I told him I wasn't interested he just hung up real quick, so I don't know any more than that."

Tiny whistles. "Yeah, I think I'd walk away from a call like that, too."

"Well, anyway, I thought it was kind of weird he'd call me after five years. I don't care enough to try to run it down, so I guess I'll let you go. Say hi to Nancy for me."

"Whoa, now," Tiny says. "Don't hang up so quick, man. I said I was getting ready to call you, remember?"

"Okay," I say. I hadn't figured I'd hear from Tiny until the wedding and honeymoon and all that stuff was over with.

"Listen, man, I got to tell you again, I'm real sorry you couldn't be on the guest list for the wedding."

I laugh. "Come on, Tiny. You and me both know Stan wouldn't even want me in the same county as his little girl when she's getting married. I figure you'd invite me if you thought you could get away with it."

"You know it. Me and Nancy talked about it and figured we'd better not even bring it up. He's a happy guy right now and Nancy wants to keep it that way."

"Makes sense to me."

"I think that's why Nancy wants to talk to Molly, explain things to her."

"She knows about the bad blood between me and Stan, so she'll understand."

We're both quiet for a minute and Tiny says, "Well, anyway, that's what I was going to call you about. I better let you go. Don't go getting mixed up in something you can't get out of."

"Yeah, my plan is to stay out of jail. I got too much going on right now I don't want to miss. See you, man."

Tiny calls me two days later.

"You see the news?"

I don't watch TV, don't read the paper, pretty much have no idea what's going on. "No. Something happen I ought to know about?"

"Your buddy Curt and a couple other guys got caught breaking into a jewelry store."

"No shit?"

"No shit. I guess I really ought to say they got caught trying to break in. Dumbasses either didn't know how the alarm system worked or thought they could get in and back out before they got caught. They never even made it inside."

Damn.

"Well, if he was in charge, I could see it. He never was worth a damn at thinking things through."

"Most criminals are stupid," says Tiny. "Guess your friend's going away for a while, since they caught them in the act."

"It say who else was in on this?"

Tiny tells me the names of the other two guys, and I sort of remember them, but not really.

"Anyway," he says, "thought you'd like to know. See you sometime."

After he hangs up I turn to Frankie. "You know how close I came to a real shitty life, girl? If it hadn't been for Gamaliel, and then Nancy and Tiny, but mostly Gamaliel, I'd probably have gotten sucked into that group, and with my luck I'd have been caught first time I tried to do anything."

I never did know why Nancy started talking to me back then, but right now I'm sure as hell glad she did.

Maybe I'll ask her the next time we see her and Tiny. I don't know when that'll be, exactly, but I figure after everything settles down we might see them some, between the wedding and the baby. After the baby comes I bet we won't see much of them at all.

I can't stop thinking about who I was when I was running around with Curt and who I am now, and there's only one person I can talk to about this.

Chapter Twenty-Five

I'm already out on the road, so instead of going home I head for Sylvia's. I know things between me and Molly aren't the best right now, but even with that, she's the one I need and I know that.

I don't call ahead or anything, just pull into the driveway and park the truck. I get Frankie out and we head toward the front door. I'm about to knock when it opens and Molly is looking up at me.

"Hi."

"Can I come in? I need to talk to you."

"Oh," she says. "Sure, come on in. Gram is gone for a while. A guy from The Commons is taking her on a tour of the place. Looks like her move is coming up pretty soon."

"That's good."

She frowns at me. "What's that supposed to mean?"

I'm not even in the door and I'm already screwing this up. I shake my head.

"I mean it's good that she's not here. I didn't mean it's good that she's going. I mean, I mean, oh, hell, Molly, I really need to talk to you. Just you. That's all I meant."

She looks at me for a long time. "Guess you'd better come on in, then."

When we get to the back of the house she rolls into her regular spot and sits there with her hands in her lap. "What did you want to talk about?"

"Curt got arrested last night."

"Who's Curt?"

"A guy from school, back in high school. He was a friend, I guess he was a friend. I didn't really have any, but I guess he was the closest thing I had to one. He used to come over sometimes. None of the other guys would, and girls, well, that never happened either. He didn't laugh at me or make fun of me, at least not to my face, and then he got a chance to start running with the older guys, the ones who were in Timmons' gang, and then I was pretty much by myself."

She doesn't say anything, but she's got her eyes on me and she's listening hard. Frankie is right next to her and Molly's stroking her head.

"That was after it was just me at the house, and I was pissed at him but I would have given anything to get in with that crew."

"I know," she says, "after your dad ran off and

your mother did too, and took Hannah with her. I can't imagine how hard that must have been, sweetie."

"That's not exactly how it happened."

"What do you mean? How what happened?"

I'm shaking like a leaf right now, and rubbing my palms on my pants, and I'm thinking you'd better not do this, but I know I'm going to, and it's scaring me to death.

"There was this big fight, not like Momma and Daddy didn't fight all the time, but mostly it'd be Daddy yelling at her and her taking it, but this time I guess she'd had it and while he was out of the house she took off to her sister Claire's and sent for Hannah, and then it was just me and Daddy."

I've been staring at the floor, but now I raise my head and look her right in the eye.

"What I'm about to tell you, I've never told anybody. Not Gamaliel, not Tiny, not even Mark. Nobody knows this, okay?"

"Okay." She's whispering, so I can barely hear her, and her eyes are wide open. She's leaning toward me now.

"Okay, that weekend, Daddy was drunk, like always, and that night he'd cracked me up the side of my head with that damn claw of a hand because I was trying to protect Momma. She was just there on the kitchen floor on her hands and knees with blood

251

running down her face, trying to clean up the broken dishes, and I went after him and he just about knocked me out.

"The next morning I got up and there was a note from Momma. She's gone, and I'm supposed to put Hannah on the school bus on Monday with her stuff so Aunt Claire can pick her up. Daddy had gone off somewhere, I didn't know where, and so I did what the note said and got her on the bus on Monday.

"I came back and his truck was there at the house and I saw him come out of the house with the shotgun and head to the barn . . ."

I have to stop for a second.

"And I heard the gun, and when I got to the barn and looked in he was laying there and blood was all over the place."

I'm afraid to look at Molly so I keep staring at my hands.

"I stood there for I don't know, a long time, and I didn't know what to do. I know I wasn't sorry not even a little bit. I was glad he was gone and he was just laying there and finally I got a shovel and went out in the field where he wanted to bury Frankie, you know my brother, when he died and the state said you can't do that, and I went out there and dug a grave out there in the field and I cleaned up the barn the best I could and drug him out there on an old tarp we had and I buried him out there in that field."

And I just sit there staring at my hands.

"I went back a few months later and put a rock where the grave was and, well, that's it."

I wait for her to say something but she doesn't.

"So I couldn't tell anybody and all I had was Gamaliel and I sure couldn't tell him, and then Nancy came up to me one day when I was at school. I was going once or twice a week so the law wouldn't come out to the house because I was too young to drop out. If it wasn't for her, and Tiny, and Gamaliel, I'd probably have done whatever to get in with Curt and that crew and I might have been with him last night and gotten arrested.

"So now you know the worst thing I've ever done. I swear I wouldn't blame you a bit if you didn't want to have anything to do with me and I wouldn't blame you if you called the law right now and they came and hauled me off. You deserve a hell of a lot better than somebody like me, that's for damn sure."

I hear a little noise, and when I look up she's on her way out of the room. Frankie comes over and leans up against my leg and we just sit there.

She's gone for a couple of minutes, but it seems like forever until she comes back in the room. She's got a couple of glasses and Sylvia's bottle of brandy in her lap, and she puts them on the table.

"I don't think Gram will mind if we have some of her brandy, do you?"

She pours a little into each glass and brings one over to me.

It's about one good swallow, and that's all it takes for both of us to empty our glasses. Molly sets hers down on the table and turns to me.

"So," she says.

She's looking at me and all I can think is why in the hell did you tell her that and ruin the absolute best thing that's ever happened to you or is ever going to happen? I'm trying to figure out a way to take it all back when she says, "So that's the worst thing you've ever done?"

I laugh. "Yeah, that's it."

She shrugs. "I'm not seeing this the same way you are, sweetie.

"After the terrible way your daddy treated you your whole life, for you to bury him where he wanted to lay his son to rest was a kind and respectful thing to do, and that's all that needs to be said about it as far as I'm concerned."

I don't get it. All these years I've carried this around, scared to death I'm going to slip up and say something, and she's treating it like I did a good deed for Daddy.

I shake my head. "I figured you'd throw my ass right out of here and tell me never to come back."

"And give back this ring? Are you crazy?" She gives me a wink and a little grin.

"Listen to me, sweetie," she says, and her voice is real serious. "You're not the only one carrying stuff around. Everybody has secrets. Everybody. I would never have known Gram's secret if she hadn't asked you what year you graduated from high school, and I've lived with her for years. The stuff that happened inside my house when I was growing up, well, maybe someday I'll tell you about some of that. I mean, look at Tiny and Nancy, how they're starting out their marriage. What you told me stays with me. I can promise you that."

I think about that night at Nancy's when they had me over for dinner and I saw Nancy's mom and dad and it was just like watching Momma and Daddy, and I knew what was going on, except it was all under the surface instead of out in the open. And they were all pretending everything was just fine. Molly's right. Everybody has secrets.

I nod. "You're something, you know that?"

"I know. Surely it hasn't taken you this long to figure that out."

She keeps a straight face until I start laughing, and then she starts in too.

Bert and Ray jump up out of their beds, and Frankie perks up her ears. We hear the door open and close, and Sylvia walks into the room. She takes one look at us and says, "Good. You've already got the brandy out. I'll get a glass for myself."

Molly starts to say something and comes over next to me instead. Sylvia pours herself a couple of swallows and holds up the bottle to us.

I nod, and Molly says, "Sure, Gram. Why not?"

She collapses into her chair and nobody says anything at first. Finally Molly says, "So, how was the grand tour?"

"It was lovely. Just lovely."

This is one of those times that I'm pretty sure I don't know what's going on. Does she mean she liked it or hated it?

Molly looks a little confused, too, and I guess Sylvia notices. She laughs a little.

"It really was a very nice tour. It's a beautiful place, and if it didn't mean leaving you I'd be ready to go tomorrow."

She finishes her drink and says, "I hate the thought of being apart from you, dear, but there are so many good things about The Commons. The staff seem to be glad to be there, the food was good, and the buildings and grounds, well, they're immaculate." She glances at me. "When I move there I won't need a landscaper, or a gardener, or a handyman."

She sighs and says, "The new units at The Commons will be ready mid-January, they tell me. That's only a couple of months away, so I need to start thinking about what to take with me and what to sell." She looks at Molly. "Have the two of you set a date yet?"

I don't know what to say to that after what I told Molly just before Sylvia got here. I'm still kind of afraid I've ruined things, but Molly says, "Not for sure, but I'm thinking middle of next month. What do you think about that, sweetie?" She turns to Sylvia. "I just now thought of that, so I'm kind of springing it on Boone right now. I'm just thinking, a wedding, Christmas, and New Year's would make a great month of celebrating."

"My goodness! You're going to wear me out!" Sylvia says, but she's smiling. They both turn to me.

I know I'm supposed to say something here. What I want to say is, you mean the wedding's still on?, but I don't want to get into all that with Sylvia here.

I nod. "The sooner the better, as far as I'm concerned."

Chapter Twenty-Six

Molly says it doesn't bother her, missing Nancy and Tiny's wedding, but I think she would have liked to be there. The only thing she said about it was, "If you're not welcome there, I wouldn't go if they asked me," which I appreciated, but I still think she would have liked it.

Tiny and Nancy both act kind of strange when we finally get around to telling them about us. That whole thing with Curt got me sidetracked, and I guess it did Molly, too, so we didn't know if they'd already heard somehow and were pissed at us.

When I call Tiny and tell him the first thing he says is, "You're a little slow, man. Nancy got the word from Molly about five minutes ago."

"I know," I say. "I was sitting right beside her. I figured ladies first. I read that somewhere, can't remember exactly where." I don't tell him Molly had a kind of a funny look on her face when she put down her phone.

"Well, congratulations," he says. He doesn't sound all that happy, and I'm trying to decide if I want to know why when he says, "You hear about our wedding?"

"No."

"I thought it might have made the papers."

"Man, you know I don't read the newspaper. So what happened?"

"Nancy's been able to keep Stan from knowing about the baby, you know, baggy sweatshirts and like that, but she wore this really nice dress for the wedding, and we were doing pictures after the ceremony and I guess it was the way she was standing or something, but he took one look at her and man, you better be glad you weren't there."

"No shit?"

"No shit. I don't know how Nancy's mom got him to finally calm down, but me and Nancy didn't even go to our own reception. It was tense, man, real tense. We haven't been to their house since, and I think Nancy's talked to her mom but I'm not even sure. The only way it could have been worse is if you'd have been there. I bet he would have figured out some way to blame you and who the hell knows how that would have ended."

When I hang up I look at Molly. "Damn."

She nods. "What an awful way to have to start out. I feel so bad for Nancy, but I think this one she's going to have to work out on her own. I wouldn't know how to help even if she'd let me."

We still need to talk about our wedding, I guess, but I remember Mark saying that my job is just to show up on time in the right place and let the bride's family do everything else.

"You're going to tell me if I need to do anything, right?" I ask Molly. We're at my place finishing off a pizza.

"Since you brought it up," she says, "let me run a few things by you and see what you think."

"Okay."

"Mark's doing the ceremony, of course. We'd never hear the end of it if we got anybody else."

"Right."

"As soon as Gram and I figure out what we're wearing, we'll let you know what you need to wear."

I never thought about that.

"You mean like a suit?"

She laughs. "My god, you should see the look on your face. Maybe so, but I promise we'll let you know as soon as we decide on that."

A suit. A damn suit. I start to say something about how stupid it is to buy something I'm never going to wear again in my life but I catch myself just in time.

"And we'll need rings. Sometime soon we need to go pick those out."

Okay. Now I'm glad I've still got some of the money Gamaliel left me.

"And you'll need somebody to be your best man."

"So what does he do?"

She looks at me like I'm a six year old, and I'm about to say something about that when she says, "I keep forgetting that you don't have a lot of experience with this. A best man stands beside you during the ceremony. He's usually a good friend or a relative. It's an honor to be asked."

"Maybe I'll get Tiny. I mean if he's up for being in another wedding after what happened at his."

"I'm trying to decide between asking Nancy and Charlotte. Most of the friends I had before the accident, well, they visited me in the hospital and maybe a couple of times after, but mostly what they did was stare at my wheelchair and feel sorry for me. Eventually they stopped coming around and I stopped trying to stay in touch. It was too painful for everybody, especially the ones who were there when it happened.

"So, anyway, we just sort of stopped being friends."

She looks really sad and I start to say something when she says, "You know, it's funny. When you were telling me all that the other day, about your dad I mean, you said you didn't really have any friends then, and now you've got some great ones. I used to have lots of friends, and now my friends are the people I've met through you."

I guess that's right. The people back at school, most of them wouldn't give me the time of day. I remember Daddy talking about a guy once, some guy he worked with and really didn't like, and he said, "That asshole wouldn't piss on you if you were on fire." There's nobody around me now that I could say that about, and it's hard for me to think of anybody I'd say that about anyway.

"I'm pretty lucky, I guess."

"It's not luck, sweetie. You're a great guy." She squeezes my hand.

"By the way, I talked to Mark and asked him to look at his calendar. He'll let us know when he can do it, maybe give us a couple of choices, and we'll go from there. Gram insists on having the ceremony at our house, and I'm fine with that if you are."

"Mark told me a while back that my job was to make sure I was at the right place at the right time, and I figure I can handle that. You just let me know where and when. I'll be there."

The next day Mark gives Molly a couple of dates to pick from and she tells him about having the ceremony at Sylvia's.

"I wanted to do it a week before Christmas, but he doesn't have the eighteenth open. So how about the nineteenth?" She's talking mostly to Sylvia but looks over at me too.

I shrug. "Whenever you want to do it is fine with me. I'm not doing a lot of work now since the weather's getting colder, so I'm good pretty much any time."

"The nineteenth it is, then. I'll call Mark."

Every time Sylvia and Molly are together now they're talking about food, or decorating, or vows. "Oh, that's right," says Molly. "I forgot to tell you. I want us to write our own vows."

I don't know exactly what she's talking about until she explains.

"Hell, I wouldn't know what to say."

"Just tell me how fantastic I am and you'll be in good shape," she says, and winks at Sylvia. "Right, Gram?"

We're just a few weeks away from this and I still haven't decided about Momma and Aunt Claire. Especially Aunt Claire.

We tell Raymond and Charlotte about the date, and Tiny and Nancy, and they can all come. Mrs. Cooperton has to clear the trip with Hannah's caseworker but she thinks it'll work okay, and Frances is planning to come. I ask Mark about Carrie and he says, "I'll have to think about that. I don't know how she's doing these days or if she's realized that Jerry's death wasn't your fault."

It takes me about a minute to change my mind

about Carrie and call Mark back. When I tell him to forget about Carrie he says, "I think that's best, Boone, and if you hadn't come to that on your own I would have suggested that you leave her off the list. She was a good friend to you, but things ended very badly, and I think a call from you would just bring everything back to the surface."

When I ask Tiny about him being my best man he's quiet for a long time. "Listen, man, you know I would have had you for mine in a heartbeat but with Stan and all . . . ."

"Hell, Tiny, I know that." I don't know that at all, and I figure he's got a lot of friends to pick from. Feels good to hear him say it, though.

"So, can you do it?"

"Damn right I can. You know this means I get to say all kinds of stuff about you at the reception, right?"

Didn't know that, either. "You'll have to keep it kind of clean. We're at Sylvia's house for the whole thing."

"Maybe I'll wait til she's out of the room before I tell the best stuff."

Chapter Twenty-Seven

"After the ceremony and the honeymoon, why don't you two just move in here?" Sylvia is having her afternoon coffee and brandy, and Molly and I are joining her. Frankie and Bert and Ray are in their beds taking their third or fourth nap of the day.

"I thought I'd better hang onto my place at least for now," I say, "since you'll be selling the house and we don't know when that's going to happen."

Everybody gets real quiet.

I don't have any idea what it's like to get attached to a place. The closest I came was when I was living at Gamaliel's old place for a while, and that was because of the old man.

Sylvia finally says, "I'm going to be saying goodbye to a lot of memories," and her voice is kind of shaky.

"Me, too, Gram," says Molly.

I don't like this everybody sitting around feeling sad stuff, but I don't know what to do about it either.

The only thing I ever felt leaving a place was glad, even Gamaliel's, but that was because of Jerry being such a prick.

Molly says, "You want us to make a video of the place so you can look at it every now and then? I can do it on the iPad you got me."

Sylvia shakes her head. "No, dear. I don't think that would be a good idea."

I got to agree with Sylvia on that.

The next day we're at my place and I sit down next to Molly.

"I can't put this off any longer."

She starts to say what are you talking about but stops and grabs hold of my hand. "She's the only one you haven't called, sweetie. If you're going to invite her to the wedding she needs to know far enough ahead of time to make plans. She's coming farther than anybody else."

"If she comes," I say. "She told me not to get married, remember? She might stay away just out of spite."

Molly sighs. "Well, you'll never know until you call her."

"Might as well get it over with."

I'm doing this because I have to. I mean, she's my mother and all, but she's the only one on my little list I don't feel good about inviting. I know it's because of what she said the last time we talked, but it still kind of pisses me off.

She picks up on the third ring.

"Hey, Momma."

Damned if she doesn't start crying right off the bat. "Oh, Boone, I'm so sorry for what I said the last time about, you know. If this little girl makes you happy, then I'm happy too."

I take a deep breath. "That's why I called you, Momma. I'd, I mean, we'd like you to come to the wedding."

Her voice changes. "So, you're really going to do it?"

"Yeah, Momma, it's going to be in December, on the nineteenth. We're having the wedding at Sylvia's. She's Molly's grandmother. And Mark is going to do the ceremony."

"That's awful quick, son. Did you get that girl in trouble?"

"No, Momma, she's not pregnant." I'm already sorry I called her, but I decide to go through with this no matter what. "We just don't see any reason to put it off now that we've decided."

"I guess I could try to get down there."

"That'd be great, Momma. You call when you know for sure and I'll give you directions."

I hang up. Molly is staring at me. I really can't tell what she's thinking.

"That settles one thing," I say.

"What's that?"

"There's no way in hell I'm going to have her and Aunt Claire in the same room at the same time. If those two really started going at it it'd be worse than Tiny and Nancy's."

Molly doesn't say anything and when I look over at her again she's a thousand miles away.

"You okay?"

She nods. "I was just thinking. Maybe I'll see if Mom and Dad would like to come. Gram can help me get hold of them." She shakes her head. "I don't know, I just don't. It's been a while since Mom and I have really talked, and more like forever for my dad." She looks at me. "What do you think I should do?"

"I'm the last person to ask about parents," I say. "But if you're thinking about it, ask Sylvia. She knows a lot more than me."

"She's got her own history with them, sweetie. But you're right, I should talk to her. I'll do that tonight. The nineteenth is just around the corner, you know."

I do know that. The closer I get to it the more scared I get. I hate carrying this around but I don't know who to go to. Tiny's probably not going to tell me how great it is and how I should go ahead with it, and I've talked Mark's ear off about everything in the world the last five or six years. He must be about worn out with my shit, and besides, he's the guy that's kind of in charge of the whole thing.

We barely notice Thanksgiving, which Molly says is usually a special meal for her and Sylvia. This time it's more like what we usually eat, but Sylvia does remember to make a pecan pie. Hers isn't as good as Mrs. Armstrong's down in New Orleans, but I'll be damned if I'm going to tell her that. It does bring back some memories that I'm not going to tell Molly about either. She knows enough already.

Sylvia eats the last bite of pie, pushes her chair back from the table, and says, "Anybody else want a cup of decaf?"

We both do, and when she's back with the coffee we just stay there at the table, talking about marriage and moving.

"After you proposed to Molly, I thought about tearing up my contract with The Commons and staying here," Sylvia says. "I thought you and Molly could just move in here with me and I could stay right where I am."

Molly starts to say something, but Sylvia holds up her hand. "I'm not going to do that, though, and I'll tell you why.

"When I went up to get the grand tour and saw all the things they have for old folks, that are set up just for us, I realized how homebound I'd become. Not because of you, dear," she says, seeing Molly's expression, "I know I don't have to be with you here every minute. I just got lazy, and then when driving became more difficult I had another reason to sit at home."

"Gram, we can take you wherever you want to go," Molly says. "Right, Boone?" but Sylvia's already shaking her head.

"At The Commons, there are all kinds of things to do that are right there on the grounds. Here," and she waves her hand around, "everything is spread out over who knows how many miles. Besides, as much as I enjoy your and Boone's company, there are good things about being around people my own age."

Molly slumps down in her chair and won't look at either one of us, but I get what Sylvia's talking about.

"You didn't have to be so quick to agree with her," Molly says later, when we're in the hallway and I'm getting ready to hit the road.

"I don't know, darlin', the way she was talking about that place made me think keeping her here would be kind of selfish."

"Oh, so I'm selfish now."

I didn't mean it like that, I tell her, but it looks like the damage is already done. She just about slams the door on Frankie's tail.

The next time I hear from her it's three days later, and she calls me in the middle of the afternoon. Frankie is asleep on one end of the couch and I'm kind of in and out on the other.

"Okay, maybe a little bit selfish," she says,

without even saying hello.

"I didn't mean it like that," I say.

"I know. I was just reacting. Can you come over to eat tonight?"

"Anytime you say."

She's quiet for a minute. "I called Mom."

I sit up. I'm almost afraid to ask, but it turns out I don't have to.

"She's coming. Says she can't wait to meet you."

I don't say anything, but I guess Molly can tell what I'm thinking.

"It'll be fine, sweetie. Mom knows I'm crazy about you. She wouldn't dare do anything to mess that up." Molly clears her throat. "The only thing I'm a little worried about is her and Gram. It was kind of tense between them right after the divorce, when I ended up here."

"Sylvia is okay with her coming?"

"More or less."

I can't imagine Sylvia being anything but kind and it's hard to picture her mad. I tell Molly that and she says, "It doesn't happen very often, but let me tell you, she knows how to be mad. Definitely."

Maybe I don't want to know what she's talking about.

When I was a kid, living with Daddy meant living with a man who was mad pretty much all the time. We all sort of figured out how to live with it, and the only thing we had to wonder about was how mad was he, was he drunk too, and who was he going to take it out on. I think it might be harder to live with somebody who almost never got mad. You'd never know it was coming.

As soon as that crosses my mind I know it's bullshit. No way living with Daddy was better than living with somebody like Sylvia.

This whole wedding thing is starting to feel like we're putting a bunch of bobcats in the same pen and trying to keep them fed and more or less calm until we can open the gate and let them all go back home.

Chapter Twenty-Eight

Sylvia is going to put the house and land up for sale in January. I'm hoping it sells quick, because I know she needs the money for The Commons, but I am not looking forward to cleaning this place out.

She and Molly started working on trying to get a handle on what to keep and what to sell about a week ago, but it wasn't long before Sylvia said, "We can't do this and plan a wedding at the same time. Besides, this is where it's going to be. We'll worry about sorting and packing after we get you two married."

Mark calls me and says he needs to talk to me and can I come down to his office. "You are certainly welcome to bring Molly along, but I have a feeling she's a little busy right now."

When Frankie and I get there Mark says, "I got a call from your Aunt Claire."

I sit down across from him in my usual spot. "So what did she say?"

"About what you would expect. She's very hurt and angry about not being invited, but when she heard your mother might be there she said she wouldn't come if you begged her."

I lean back. "That's good. I got to tell you, Mark, I was dreading having to deal with the two of them if they got into it. Which they would. There's real bad blood there now."

He nods. "The fantasy a lot of people have about weddings is of the entire family setting aside their differences for a few hours and coming together to wish the new couple well, but the reality is seldom like that."

"Did you hear about Tiny's wedding?"

"I did. Very sad, that they are beginning their lives together under that cloud. That was a big secret they tried to keep from Nancy's father, though. Even if they had pulled it off, the arrival of his grandchild so soon after the ceremony would surely have tipped Stan off to the circumstances that led to their rush to marriage."

"Tiny was just trying to do the right thing, man. He could have taken off, or tried to say it wasn't his kid."

"True. I'm not faulting either Tiny or Nancy, except maybe their decision to put their trust in birth control instead of waiting." He looks at me. "You and Molly are moving kind of fast, too."

"Molly and I, we haven't done it yet. We talked about kids, and maybe sometime later, but not right now." There's no way I'm telling Mark about Sylvia and why she had to drop out of school, but I figure he's trying to ask about me and Molly without coming right out and asking.

"That's good," he says. I'm hoping he's going to change the subject, and he does.

"I really wanted to talk about your upcoming marriage. It's completely normal to have second thoughts about a decision of this magnitude, especially with the stance your mother took when you told her you were thinking about proposing. How are you, Boone? Any doubts you want to talk about? Having second thoughts?"

I shake my head, but the truth is I'm scared shitless. He just waits, and in about a minute I say, "Okay, this whole thing has me scared. I'm not worried about Molly. She's the one for me, no doubt about it. It's just so damn big, and permanent, and, you know, public."

"It is, all of those things. Let me say this, Boone. I've known you for several years now, and you have made some pretty bad decisions, and a lot of very good ones. More good than bad, in my opinion, and you don't tend to make the same bad decision more than once. The good ones, you're getting better at, and may I say that your decision to marry Molly is the best one you've made in the time I've known you. She is a remarkable young woman and is also head over heels in love with you."

"I know. I got no idea how I lucked into this."

"Me neither." He laughs. "I don't see this kind of thing very often, but I do love it when it comes around." He leans over the desk. "You know you can come to me anytime, if you need to talk about this or anything else."

After a minute I say, "There's one other thing I am definitely going to need your help on."

"What's that?"

"Molly wants us to write our own vows."

"She told me she was thinking about that when we talked about possible dates for the ceremony. If you want to write down some thoughts and let me look at them I'll do that. I would be glad to help, but as I remember your speech at Gamaliel's funeral, I believe you'll need less help than you think. Just speak from the heart, Boone, and tell the truth. You'll be fine. No, better than fine."

"Thanks." I don't believe him, not for a minute. I'm not sure I can go through with this. Maybe if we were just going to run up to the courthouse and have some random judge do it, okay, but in front of all these people, I just don't know.

Mark sees the look on my face and says, "What's on your mind right now?"

When I tell him he says, "Okay, let's see who we've got coming. I'll be there, and you, and Molly, and Sylvia."

"Raymond and Charlotte, Tiny and Nancy," I say. "Tiny's going to be my best man. Molly says her mom is coming. Frances is going to be there, and Hannah and Mrs. Cooperton. Momma is a big maybe. Who knows what she's going to do."

"Anybody else?"

"Molly is thinking about her dad, but she says it's been forever since she's seen him and she doesn't even know where he is."

"So about a dozen people, more or less. Except for Molly's mother and Mrs. Cooperton, all these people know you, Boone, and we all love you."

It still makes me feel funny when he talks like this.

"Now listen, Mark, if you start saying that kind of shit during the ceremony I'll get all red faced and probably won't be able to get two words out."

"I make no promises, Boone, but I'll try to restrain myself as much as I can."

He's enjoying this, I can tell.

"I'm thinking it would have been better if you'd just sprung it on me that day, like you did when you got me up there to talk about Gamaliel."

"It's a little too late for that, unfortunately."

"Yeah, I know," I say. I can't think of anything

else I need to talk to him about, and after we sit there for a few minutes he says, "If you're sure you're okay, Boone, I've got a meeting coming up in about a half hour that I need to get ready for."

A couple of days later I'm finishing up what's probably going to be the last job I do before the wedding and when I go out to my truck Tiny is standing there. "Are you about to finish up here?" he says.

"Just need to get paid and I'm done."

"Good. I'll follow you home so you can take a quick shower and get Frankie settled in. We're going shopping."

I just look at him.

"Molly called me. She and Sylvia have decided what you and me are supposed to wear."

"Damn, Tiny, I can't see spending a bunch of money on something I'm never going to use again. I mean, what do I do with a suit? Can't wear it on any job I've ever had, and the places we go when we're out to eat or whatever, nobody's that dressed up."

"We're good, man. Molly and Sylvia know they'd never get you into a suit, so we are going to get long sleeved white shirts and dark blue pants. The big thing is we need to match, and that's why I'm taking you to the store."

"Look at us," Tiny says. We're standing next to each other looking into one of those full-length mirrors. I got to say we look pretty good.

"I just don't understand why all the women in this store aren't lined up to ask us what we're doing this Saturday night," he says, grinning.

"I couldn't tell you, man," I say.

"A couple of manly men, no doubt in my mind," says Tiny. "If Molly sees you looking like this before the wedding she'll be all over your ass. Won't even bother trying to get you into a bedroom."

"Shit," I say, but I do kind of like that idea.

When I get home I realize I don't have any hangers. All my clothes I just fold up and put on a shelf or in a drawer, or mostly just leave them on the floor wherever I am when I change. I've seen Molly's closet, and when we're living together I figure I'll get about a foot of closet space, but at least she's got a lot of hangers.

I've never lived with anybody before.

I mean, except when I was a kid. I don't really count that, and I've been on my own ever since I was sixteen.

I think about the two weeks at Raymond and Charlotte's place, and wonder if that's what it's going to be like. Probably not, since we had the two of them to eat with and talk to and all that. Molly's had that with Sylvia, but it's just been me and Frankie for a long time.

"You know," I say to Frankie, "Me and Molly, we

haven't really talked about any of this living together stuff."

Now I'm really getting scared.

I don't know how money's going to work. I mean, for just me and Frankie, I'm doing fine, but having Molly is going to make it more expensive to go to the store, or go out to eat, or anything.

I look around the house we're in. I guess it's going to be okay for Molly. It's good for me and Frankie, but I've seen how many books she's got. I don't know where we'd put them all. It's not like we have a library like Charlotte does.

She can't drive, and she's going to want to go up and see Sylvia a lot, at least at first. In the winter that'll be fine, since I'm not working all that much, but when it warms up it'll be different.

I've only had to take her to the doctor's once or twice, but that's more than I've ever gone. Is she going to need a lot of special medicines and stuff like that?

I wonder if Tiny and Nancy got all this worked out before they got married. Probably not, since they had the kid coming. They just had to get it done as quick as they could.

Damn, I am not ready for this.

Chapter Twenty-Nine

I answer the phone and it's Raymond. "Is there room at your house to park Big Blue?"

"I think so. It'll be tight, but I think you can do it. Maybe if you let Charlotte drive."

He laughs. "I will certainly pass that on. She will appreciate the compliment. If you can give me your address, we will see you in one or two days, depending on how many stops we make along the route."

"You're on the road already? The wedding's not for a couple of weeks."

"We are indeed, but we will not be taking a direct route to your home. The open square in Asheville is surrounded by restaurants and shops and is a favorite of Charlotte's, and we are going there first. We are looking forward to this visit and especially the celebration, Boone. See you soon."

This is really happening. I guess since they are already on their way it's too late to back out now, but

I still have a bunch of stuff I need to get straight with Molly about.

When I see Molly the next day I tell her I need about two hours with her over at my place.

"Is everything okay?"

"Yeah, I just want to talk to you about some stuff."

Before I go get her I try to make a list of things. Money, doctors, closet space. That's as far as I get before I start thinking this is really stupid. I'm about ready to call it off but I decide to just start and see what happens.

"You want an S&S?"

"Sure." She looks worried. "You're scaring me a little, sweetie."

I bring the drinks in from the kitchen and sit beside her on the couch. "I'm sorry, I don't want to scare you. There's some stuff, I mean, some things we haven't talked about and I just think, I mean, don't you think we ought to talk about it before, you know, before the wedding?"

She takes a sip and then a long drink. She sets the glass on the arm of the couch and says, "I don't know what this is all about, but if you're getting ready to call this off I guess now is better than the day of."

I knew I'd screw this up. "No, no, I'm not wanting to do that. I'm scared as hell but I still want to do it. But we haven't talked about some stuff and I figure we ought to."

"Okay, why don't you start?"

She's all tense and her face is real tight. I decide to just jump in and hope it works out.

"Well, money. We haven't talked about money." She doesn't say anything. "And doctors. And closet space."

She starts laughing then, and I don't know whether to be mad at her for laughing at me or glad she's not mad anymore.

"God, sweetie, you had me so worried that you had changed your mind. By all means, let's talk about all those things. And children, and religion, and politics, and anything else you want to talk about."

I take a deep breath. "Okay. That's good. So, I make enough money to take care of me and Frankie, but I figure that it won't be enough for the three of us."

She waves her hand. "My SSI check will take care of a lot of that."

The look on my face probably lets her know I don't have any idea what an SSI is.

She points to the wheelchair. "I get a little check from the government every month because I'm a handicapped person and unable to be a member of the work force. I guess it's so I can buy things, help the economy, something. I don't know exactly."

I'll be damned. I didn't know the government did

that kind of stuff.

"How big is the check?"

"I get $600.00 a month. Right now it goes right into Gram's checking account since I'm living with her, but we'll be changing that as soon as we have a marriage license to prove we're married."

I fall back on the couch. "So I got myself all worked up for nothing."

"Yeah."

"Why didn't you tell me about the money?"

"You never asked. Gram thinks it's because you're too much of a gentleman. I can't wait to tell her it's because you didn't know such a thing existed."

It gets easier after that.

Molly laughs all the way through the closet space thing. "I promise to give you at least a foot of space to hang up all your fancy clothes."

Politics and religion are a little weird. I don't know anything about politics except that it's the government and as far as I can tell it's a bunch of rich people trying to tell us what to do, and taking money from us every chance they get. Molly asks me if I'm a Democrat or a Republican and I say, "I don't know. Do I have to choose?" She thinks for a minute and says, "I guess not."

Talking to Mark's all the religion I need, and when I tell her that she says, "Well, Gram and I have this church we really like. We've been going for years, but with her moving I guess I'll have to figure out what I'm going to do about that."

She wants to have kids, one or two, and I tell her that what scares me more than anything about that is what I know about being a father is what I saw Daddy doing, and I know that's not the right way to do it. He showed me how to be a bad one. What I don't know is, how to be a good one.

"Oh, sweetie," she says, laying her hand on my arm, "you don't have to worry about that. We'll do just fine when the time comes."

"Damn, I sure hope so," I say.

When I call Mark the next day and tell him about the talk he says, "Once again you're a step ahead of me. I was planning to call you and ask if you and Molly could meet with me for a little pre-marriage counseling. That offer is still open, if you think you need it. If you have some things you didn't get to last night."

"I told you about the letters, right?"

"The ones Frances wrote to Hannah and your mother?"

"Right. I'm thinking about asking Frances if she wants to give them the letters in person or just toss them since she's going to see them and can talk to them while they're here. At least she can talk to Hannah. Still don't know about Momma."

We're less than two weeks away now, and I don't

see much of Molly. She and Sylvia are about as happy as I've ever seen two people. They're always talking about food, or decorations, or how to arrange the house to have the wedding and the reception in the same place.

"We need to have a dinner for everybody a day or two before the nineteenth," Molly says.

I don't have room at my place, and besides, my cooking is pretty much frozen pizza and stuff like that.

"If we have it two days ahead we could have it here." Sylvia is writing some kind of list and says that without even looking up.

"Gram, you'll be too worn out to walk me down the aisle if we add that to all the other stuff we're doing here."

"I know, dear, but Boone's house is too small and Mark's chapel is too far away."

"What about the church that you two go to?" I ask.

"I thought about that," says Sylvia. "Since we're not using them for the ceremony I'd feel a little funny asking them to use their fellowship hall, and they might object to us having wine with dinner and for toasting. They're pretty strict about that kind of thing.

"Let's do it here," she goes on. "Since I'm going to be leaving this place next month, I'd like for my final memories of here to be good ones, and I can't imagine better memories than these."

Raymond calls a couple of days later.

"We are on the road from Asheville and should arrive by mid-afternoon." I give him the address and tell him I'll be sure and be at home when they get there.

Charlotte makes a big fuss over Frankie when they get Big Blue parked, and I got to say it's good to see the two of them again.

They've got a tiny little car attached to the back of the RV that I've never seen before. When I ask Raymond about it, he says, "We would like to explore this area while we are here, since we have a few days, and I bought this Smart Car two months ago. It is perfect for that kind of thing."

I've never heard of a Smart Car, and it looks kind of like Mark's Mini had a baby. It's barely big enough for the two of them.

"We must visit your good friend Mark while we are here," he says. "I do not want my only interaction with him to be at the ceremony, when he will certainly be very busy."

"I can call him right now," I say.

Mark says that tomorrow would be a good day, and I tell him we'll be down around mid-morning.

I lead the way with Frankie, and Raymond and Charlotte follow in their tiny little car. I can't wait for Mark to see this thing.

The whole trip down I'm trying to remember what I've told Mark about them and what I've told them about Mark. I like all three of them, so I should be okay, but I know I say stuff without even thinking about it sometimes.

Betty barely speaks to me when I see her in the hallway. She says hello to the three of us and tells us Mark is in his office, and walks away before we can say anything.

Raymond looks at me, eyebrows raised. "Did we inadvertently say something to offend her?"

I shake my head. "I'd say it has nothing to do with you two at all."

He looks like he's going to ask me something else, but instead he says, "Let us go meet Mark. I am looking forward to greeting this man who has done so much for you."

Raymond, Charlotte and Mark hit it off from the first minute, which doesn't surprise me, and pretty soon I'm just sitting back and listening. The story about the picture is just as embarrassing as it was when Mark told Molly about it. When Mark is finished Raymond glances over at me and then nods to Mark.

"He is a fine young man, there is no question about it."

"Okay, that's it," I say, and stand up. "I'm going to get coffee. Any of y'all want some?"

Everybody does, and I kind of half expect Charlotte to offer to help me, but she just says, "Bring some extra cream, if you don't mind. I like to make little adjustments after my first sip."

I have to find a tray and poke around in the cafeteria for cream and sugar. There are some kind of sweet buns left from breakfast so I grab a plate and a few of them. I get everything on the tray and I'm almost out the door when Betty comes in.

She stops as soon as she sees me. I have my hands full with the tray but I nod and say, "How's it going, Betty?"

She starts to say something and then, just like that, she's back out in the hallway. The way the double doors are swinging back and forth, it sure looks like she tried to slam them and it didn't work.

I think about going after her, but I take the coffee back to Mark's office instead. When I get back the three of them are talking, but they stop as soon as I walk in.

"I sure would like to know what the hell's going on here," I say. "I just ran into Betty and she looked like she was ready to cuss me up one side and down the other, but she ran off down the hall instead. Then I come in here and you guys all shut up like I can't hear what you're talking about." I look down at Frankie. "Maybe Frankie and me ought to get on out of here."

Raymond starts to say something, but Mark holds up his hand. "Let's have some coffee, Boone, and I'll tell you as much as I can."

I don't like it, but I put the tray down in the spot he's cleared out on his desk. After we all have a cup, he says, "The two things have nothing to do with each other. Raymond and Charlotte and I were discussing some, well, some surprises we have in store for you and Molly. You understand I can't say any more than that.

"Betty, well," he tilts his head at Raymond and Charlotte and looks at me, "how much do they know about your experiences before your encounter in the swamp?"

"We certainly do not want to intrude on what appears to be a private issue," says Raymond.

"No," I say, "don't worry about that, Raymond. He's talking about Nancy, and you two know just about everything about me and her."

Mark nods. "Betty was at the wedding of Tiny and Nancy and witnessed Stan's blowup when he realized why the wedding had been rushed. She can't quite bring herself to accept what happened, and so, as she told me the other day, she assumes that Nancy was led astray by someone other than Tiny."

I stare at him. "She's saying it's my fault that they screwed around and Nancy got pregnant?" Raymond clears his throat and when I look at Charlotte her face is red. "Sorry, Charlotte, I could have probably said that better."

"You don't need to apologize, Boone," she says. "It just reminded me of a similar situation that happened to someone I know."

Mark jumps in. "I think this is difficult for Betty. Even though Boone worked here and was a good and valuable employee, she has connections and loyalties that predate her relationship with Boone. She is struggling right now."

Raymond nods. "That was very well said, Mark. I can see why Boone values your friendship and insights so highly. As far as the situation with Tiny and Nancy goes, let me just say that Charlotte and I have been around the block a few times, so to speak. We are neither shocked nor inclined to judgment regarding whatever indiscretions may have taken place."

Mark laughs out loud. "Have you ever considered a career as a diplomat, Raymond?"

"Oh, Mark, you should hear him when he gets going," Charlotte says. "That was just off the cuff."

Everybody but me seems to be pretty relaxed, so I'm thinking maybe I ought to just let it go. It still bothers the hell out of me that I'm nothing but white trash to her, and all it took was something happening to the daughter of one of her friends, that hadn't even been my girlfriend for a good long time. I guess I'm never going to be able to crawl out from under this thing Daddy laid on me.

Mark's reading my mind again, like he does. Sometimes it kind of freaks me out that he can do that. He says, "Boone, you can't control what kind of stories other people are going to create, especially if they're dodging something painful or uncomfortable. Everyone in this room, and a lot more as well, knows that the disaster at Tiny and Nancy's wedding had nothing to do with you." He leans toward me. "We all know what kind of man you are. If Betty or anybody else tries to disparage you to avoid the truth, that's their loss. Don't let it be yours as well."

I give him a look. "You got to stop using those big words, Mark. I don't know what they mean, and I'm afraid to guess." I turn to Raymond. "He's as bad as you are."

"He's got you there, Ray," smiles Charlotte.

"If I am being compared to Mark here, I will take that as a compliment."

Chapter Thirty

Raymond and Charlotte take the grand tour of Corey's big project and they're polite, like they always are, but neither one of them gets real excited about it.

The first time they meet Tiny and Nancy, I'm a little worried because of that thing with Betty when we went to visit Mark. I should have known better. The six of us go down to Market Square in Knoxville, and Charlotte wants us to try the Tomato Head. There's a Tupelo Honey in Asheville, she says, and she'd never even heard of Tomato Head.

It's our first time there, too, and I got to say the pizza is pretty damn good. We spend a little time walking around, watch the ice skaters for a minute or two, and then head for a coffee shop we passed on our walk to get something hot to drink and some desserts. It's the kind of day I never had before, not even with Nancy, and I'm really enjoying it.

After we take Molly back home and pick up

Frankie, we get to my place and Charlotte says, "I'm going to read for a bit and turn in. I imagine the two of you will be talking til the wee hours."

The next night me and Frankie are at Sylvia's and Raymond and Charlotte are back down in Knoxville having a look around downtown.

"I just can't get over what fine people Raymond and Charlotte are," says Sylvia.

"Told you," says Molly. "They're the best, really."

"Do you know what their plans are after the wedding?" Sylvia takes a second helping of fried okra and passes the bowl around. "Will they be going back home?"

"I don't know, and I'm not sure they do either," I say. "They like to do some planned trips and some just, you know, pick a direction and start driving."

After dessert Sylvia says, "Boone, Molly and I have been making plans and we realized last night that it's been a while since we got you up to date.

"Since we're not having a wedding shower, we think a nice dinner, probably on the seventeenth, would give everybody a chance to bring their wedding gifts instead of trying to fit everything into the day of the wedding."

I don't know what a wedding shower is and I'm kind of surprised that people will be bringing us stuff. I guess I never really thought about it.

"Sure, that's fine. We ought to let Frances and

Mrs. Cooperton and Momma know so they can be here for that. Everybody else is already in town."

Molly nods. "I thought I'd call everybody tomorrow and tell them about it."

I start to say something and she says, "If you're getting ready to offer to call them, don't. Your job is to be here on time for all this stuff and make sure you have your vows written. The rest of it is up to us."

"Okay," I say.

"Does Tiny know which jewelry store we ordered the rings from? You two should go together to pick them up, but he's in charge of bringing them to the ceremony."

When Tiny and I pick up the rings he takes one look at them and says, "Damn, Boone, these are about the prettiest things I've ever seen. Where did they come from?"

He picks up one of the rings and holds it up to the window. The walnut ring has gold edges that flash in the light. I turn to the jeweler. "That's some real nice work there."

He smiles. "I'm glad I had a couple of samples in the case when you and your fiancée came in. The look on her face when she saw them . . . ."

"I know. I'm real glad she liked the look of them. I think they're pretty damn nice myself."

On the way home Tiny says, "Nancy's going to be jealous as hell when she sees Molly's ring."

I grin at him. "And I'm real glad that's not my problem."

We ride along a little without saying anything and I turn to him. "Molly says I'm supposed to write my own wedding vows. I don't know how to even start doing that."

He shrugs. "Tell her you love her, can't live without her, you know, stuff like that." He looks over at me. "You know nobody's going to be paying any attention to you, don't you? This thing is all about Molly."

"Good to know, but I still got to say something."

"You'll figure it out. Get Mark to help you. He says stuff in public for a living, man, he could probably write you some in his sleep."

"Okay, number one, he wouldn't do it, already told me I'm going to be fine, blah, blah. Number two, if he did help me, Molly would know after the first two or three words it wasn't from me and she'd smack me silly."

Things are moving real fast now. Molly tells me that Mark is going to meet Frances and Hannah and Mrs. Cooperton the day of the dinner and take them out to lunch. First thing I think of is the letter and I call Mark about it.

"Hey, man, I haven't had a chance to give Hannah Frances' letter, and Molly tells me you're going to take them out to lunch. Do you want me to run the letter down to you so you can hand it back to Frances?"

He's quiet for a minute and then says, "That's a good idea, although she might decide to just tear it up if she can meet Hannah face to face. If you can get it down here in the next day or so I'll take it with me. Frances can decide what she wants to do when she gets here."

I take the letter down to Mark's and pass Betty in the hall. Neither one of us says a word, and she kind of speeds up when she passes me.

Mark says, "Did you see Betty?" I nod, and he shakes his head.

"She isn't going to let this go for a while, I'm afraid. So, if you've got a minute?"

"Sure."

I grab a seat, Frankie goes to her regular spot, and Mark sits behind his desk.

"I think Frances and Mrs. Cooperton and Hannah are going to stay in a motel while they're in town. I've offered to find places for them all, but they think it might be best if they weren't underfoot during all the prep."

He looks at me. "Heard from your mother?"

"No. I'm thinking she's not going to show."

"I'm sorry, Boone."

I'm not sure I am, and I tell him so. "Maybe if I hear from her I'll get her address and mail Frances' letter to her."

"Did you finish reading yours?"

"No," I say. "Can't make myself do it."

We talk for a few more minutes, and he lays out how the ceremony is going to go.

"Got your vows written yet?"

"Yeah, but they sound really lame. I don't like any part of them."

I stand up then. I don't want to talk to Mark about these stupid vows I've written that sound like some ten year old did it.

"We better get going before Betty finds a reason to throw us out."

Chapter Thirty-One

The day of the dinner I can't make myself sit still. Frankie watches me pace for a while and then goes to sleep. She's got it easy, I think.

Tiny and I meet over at Sylvia's around noon and start moving furniture around. The sun room, just off the kitchen, is going to be where the dinner is and also the ceremony, so we'll have to do some rearranging the day between. For now we're putting up four of those six foot tables that Sylvia borrowed from her church, and getting the chairs set up. One of the tables has room for Molly to roll up and she says, "Do another spot the same way for Frances."

I stop and turn to her. "Is she using a chair now?"

"Some of the time," Molly says. "She said she didn't want to be a bother, and I had to remind her that we'll be setting it up for me and can do the same for her pretty easy."

When everything's ready Molly shoos us out. "Gram and I will be cooking all afternoon, and you guys will just be in the way."

"Want me to send Nancy over?" Tiny says.

"She'll be here about an hour ahead of time."

"Okay. She didn't mention that."

"She called and offered to help," Molly says, "and that's about the time we could use an extra pair of hands."

Molly follows us down the hall, and grabs my hand to slow me down. Tiny keeps going out the door, and she looks up at me and says, "Have you ever seen Gram look this happy?"

I shake my head.

"I'm really glad you were okay with having it here," she says. "I was a little worried, but she was right. This is the best way for us to say goodbye to this house."

Me and Tiny get there a little early to direct parking, and people start coming in just a few minutes after we get there.

Raymond and Charlotte drive up in their car and Tiny starts laughing. "Damn, I thought Mark's car was little."

"You didn't see it when we had dinner together the other night?"

He shakes his head. "Nancy and I barely got there in time to eat, remember? I think they'd been looking around the square for a while already, and even if we'd parked next to that little thing we wouldn't have known it was theirs."

Mark has Frances with him. "How did she get here?" I ask him once he's got her chair unloaded and she's settled in.

"Believe it or not, Arthur drove her to the motel," says Mark. "He called me and asked if I could make sure she got around all right while she's here. He'll come by after the ceremony and pick her up."

Well, I'll be damned. "So you two are okay now?"

He frowns a little. "I wouldn't say that exactly. He likes Frances a lot, though, and I guess he's willing to tolerate a little interaction with me given the circumstances."

It's starting to get crowded by the time everybody's here, and we're almost ready to start eating when there's a knock at the door.

"I've got it," says Molly, and she's off down the hallway. She opens the front door and I hear Momma say, "I'm looking for Sylvia Wallsmith's house?"

"You found it," says Molly. "Come right in. Are you Boone's mother?"

"Yes, I am, and this is my friend Rikki."

"I am so glad you could come. I'm Molly."

There's a long silence.

"Won't you come in?" I can tell from Molly's voice that something's not right. I head down the hallway and meet them just inside the door.

"I'll go set a couple of extra places," Molly says,

and she's gone.

Momma and I look at each other for what seems like a real long time. Finally she says, "You look real good, son. Real good."

"So do you, Momma." I turn to Rikki. "I heard y'all talking before I got here. You're Rikki?" She nods. "I thank you for what you're doing for Momma, and for helping her get here and all."

Rikki smiles. "Your mother's a great gal, Boone. Listen, I left something in the car. I'll be right back." She heads out the door and it's just me and Momma standing there.

"So," I say. "You met Molly already. When Rikki gets back I'll take you on in and introduce you to everybody else."

Momma's staring at me with a real weird expression on her face. She takes a deep breath and says, "Yeah, I met Molly. That's the girl you're planning to marry?"

"Day after tomorrow. I'm real glad—"

She cuts me off. "You didn't tell me she was a cripple."

It takes me a few seconds to decide what to do.

I can feel that old anger flare up, white hot, and it takes ahold of me for just a flash. I start to lean forward and whisper something real mean in her ear, like I did with Nick back at Tiny's place when he had that cookout, but I can't make myself do it. Then it's gone, and I look Momma right in the eyes.

What I see there makes me want to cry or something. I swear it looks like she wants me to go after her like Daddy used to do. I tell myself that can't be right. Nobody would want that.

I wish Mark was here with me. Or Gamaliel. Or Raymond. I'm out here all by myself and I don't like it.

What I really wish is for Molly to be here, right beside me, but I'm also glad she isn't here to hear what my Momma just said.

"Well?" she says. "You didn't think that was important enough to tell me?"

And that's all I need to hear.

"No, Momma," I say. "It's not. It's not important at all. She's the best there is, no doubt about it, and if you give yourself a chance to see it you'll understand why I'm marrying her."

She shakes her head.

"I sure hope you know what you're doing, son. I got to say I don't think you do."

I hear Rikki coming up to the door. When she opens it I say, "Come on in and see everybody. There's plenty of food, and Frances and Hannah are both here already."

Rikki starts down the hall, but Momma hangs back. "Is Claire in there?"

I shake my head.

All of a sudden she looks scared. "Maybe I shouldn't've come here, son."

"Don't be silly," says Rikki. "We talked about this on the way down, remember?"

"I'm glad you're here, Momma," I say. "Come on. I've got some friends here I want you to meet."

We're just a couple of steps down the hall when Sylvia comes up to us.

"Hello, and welcome to my home. I'm Sylvia, Molly's grandmother. Molly has offered her room as a more private place if you want to spend a few minutes with Hannah and Frances before meeting everyone else." She takes Momma's arm and moves toward Molly's room.

I'm watching them and I can see Momma's shoulders start shaking a little bit before she even goes in.

Rikki touches my arm. "Thanks for being so nice to her, Boone. She's been worried sick all the way down here."

I start to say, if she was so worried how come she said those things about Molly, but I just don't see the use of it.

"So, you're Momma's supervisor or something?"

She laughs. "Not exactly. She's doing really good, Boone. They love her at the bakery, and she has done a lot of work getting past Jake and, of course, your father." She stops for a second. "Sorry, I shouldn't have said that."

I laugh. "Unless Momma has told you a whole lot, you don't know how bad it was. I'm real glad he's gone."

Rikki nods. "She's told me quite a bit. I think I'd like to meet your friends, if you don't mind, and give Natalie some time with her kid."

Everybody's already talking and laughing when we come in, and I take Rikki to Mark first and say, "Can you introduce Rikki around? I want to check on Momma."

"If I could make a suggestion," he says. "Maybe give them a few more minutes? Sylvia's handling that situation just fine. I think Molly and Nancy might need some help with the food."

I walk into the kitchen and Molly says, "It's about time you got here." She gives me a wink. "Gram seems to have abandoned us, and you're going to have to step in."

Nancy points to the oven. "There's a tenderloin in there that needs to come out and rest for about five minutes and then get sliced. Here," and she tosses me two potholders. "Just put it on top of the stove and cover it with aluminum foil. And turn off the oven. We're done with it."

The top of the stove is the only open spot, and as soon as I get it out and covered they give me another job. It goes like that for ten or fifteen minutes, and then Hannah comes running into the kitchen.

Sylvia's right behind her and looks around. "Okay, Boone, Molly, get out of here. Nancy, if you could give me another few minutes we'll be ready to get started."

"The tenderloin isn't sliced," I say, and she waves me off. "I have this under control, Boone. Take your bride-to-be and go mingle."

Chapter Thirty-Two

"I would like to propose a toast," Raymond says after everybody gets quiet. He's been tapping on his glass, trying to get people's attention, but it's been hard.

"Before we begin the celebration of the upcoming union of these two fine young people," he bows to me and Molly, "I believe we must raise our glasses to Sylvia, our host and chef, for a most excellent meal."

We all raise our glasses to Sylvia, who is as red as I've ever seen her. She half stands up and makes a little bow and sits back down.

Tiny stands up and says, "Okay, time to get down to business here. I'm the best man, and I'd like to start out by saying I'm glad that Boone is finally admitting that."

I lean over to Molly. "This is going to be bad."

She grins. "I know, and I can't wait."

"I met Boone when my mom told me to go down to Gamaliel's house and check on a kid that was staying there while the old man was in the hospital." He stops. "I'm real sorry Gamaliel couldn't be here with us. I bet he knows a bunch of good stories about Boone. No doubt if he was still around he'd be the best man and I'd be lucky to get invited. Even though there was that time he shot Boone and all Boone was trying to do was run off some lowlifes getting ready to rob the old man.

"Boone was pretty rough around the edges back then, and I guess I was too. We had some good times together, and some pretty tense ones. You still got that scar from the knife fight?" I nod, and he says, "Yeah, Boone had Nancy call me in, just in case he needed some help, but I got to tell you, Boone's kind of a badass. Sorry, Mark," he grins at Mark, who just waves his hand at Tiny.

"Anyway, I'm going to skip over some of the stories I could tell, because I might need to have something down the line to blackmail Boone with. You know what I'm talking about, brother," and he grins at me.

"There is one story I have to tell, about an old rifle Boone got from Gamaliel. He brought it to me and asked me to find out if it's worth anything or not, and a few months later, of course, I hadn't done a thing about it. He said that since he didn't know anything about antique guns or rebuilding them or anything I should just take it as a gift from him.

"I found out later it was a pretty valuable gun and tried to get him to take some money from me. I was going to get a few thousand out of it, and he said, 'I gave it to you, man. A gift's a gift.' A man of his word, right there," and he points to me.

"We were both kids first time I met Boone, and I've seen him turn into a man, one that I'm proud to call my best friend. Here's to you, Boone," and he raises his glass.

Nancy stands up. "My turn." She looks at Molly.

"The first time I saw you, number one, I didn't like you very much, and number two, you kind of freaked me out with the whole chair thing. And that's on me." She has to stop for a second, and grabs hold of Tiny's hand.

"It didn't get a lot easier, to tell you the truth, the next two or three times. Boone and Tiny are so close, but I couldn't figure out how to, you know, be friends with you."

She puts her hand on her stomach. "When you found out I was pregnant, you didn't hesitate a minute. You called me and said if I needed somebody to talk to, you would do that anytime. I said how about right now? and you said, okay."

She pauses again, takes a deep breath, and says, "That, saying just that one word 'okay,' was the finest thing anybody had done for me in a long time, maybe ever. You didn't have to do that, and you didn't think twice about offering. I've grown to love you like a sister. You are one of the classiest people I know, and Boone," she looks over at me, "I'm glad you had enough sense to finally ask her. She's high quality, and you are definitely marrying up." She raises her glass. "To Molly."

Molly has tears in her eyes, and I look around the room. Everybody is smiling and applauding, and I see a woman I don't know in the back with tears running down her face. She's got to be Molly's mother, I realize, and I don't know how I missed getting introduced. Maybe she got here late and I was already tied up with Momma or food or something.

Raymond stands up next, and I'm thinking this one's gonna go on for a while, but he surprises me. "I would like to say just a few words at present. I will have more to say later on, I assure you. I met Boone and Frankie in the parking lot of the Okefenokee Swamp in Georgia, where I was being accosted by three thugs, and was saved from at best a beating and at worst my possible demise by their immediate and fearless intervention. They are an extraordinary pair. Boone and Frankie, I salute you."

I lean over to Molly. "I don't get it. He's never made a speech that short in his life, I'll bet."

"Hush," she says. "Charlotte's up next."

"Dear Molly," she says. "I can't tell you what an amazing thing it is that the two of you found each other. It reminds me of myself and Ray, and that is a very good thing. We both dearly love spending time with you and Boone, and the fact that you love and appreciate books as much as I do has been an unexpected and welcome bonus. I wish the two of you as much adventure and happiness as Ray and I have found."

Mark stands up and says, "I'm going to tell one story about Boone and wrap this up. We have some gifts for the young couple and it's already getting kind of late."

He reaches down and I'll be damned if he doesn't haul the picture from his office wall off the floor and prop it on the table in front of him.

"This collage was given to me by my brother when I graduated from seminary. It's a group of ordinary people, not a famous or even recognizable face in the bunch, who lived their lives outside the spotlight. The common thread among them is that, when faced with a decision, they chose to do the right thing. Big decisions, small ones, their habit was to help, encourage, forgive, lift up the people around them.

"None of them were perfect, of course, but they all made it a point of trying to do the right thing, over and over. As I told Boone when he asked about the story behind the picture, it's no big deal until you add it all up. Then it's maybe the biggest deal there is.

"I have seen Boone live by that, stumbling

through mistakes and learning from all of them, and this picture of him and Frankie was the first one I added to the group."

He looks over at me. "When I get too preachy, he calls me on it, and I know he's going to do the same when I say this. Living the kind of life I'm talking about is doing the Lord's work here on earth."

He winks at me. "I'm going to shut up now before you shut me up, Boone. We've got to get to the gifts so we can all go home and get ready for day after tomorrow."

I know I'm as red faced as Sylvia was earlier, and I'm kind of afraid to look around. Molly punches me in the side and whispers, "Look at that, sweetie."

She nods her head, and I glance up real quick. Everybody is smiling and wiping their eyes, and I lean across the table to Tiny and say, "Do something, man. This is embarrassing."

Tiny nods, but he doesn't get up right away. When he does, he says, "There's a table right over there for any gifts y'all brought for Boone and Molly. Raymond and I have to explain ours, so we're going to ask them to go ahead and open them."

He hands me an envelope. "Nancy and I got this for you. It's actually mostly for Molly, so you ought to let her open it."

I pass it over to her and she takes it, looking at Nancy. Nancy has a huge smile on her face, and watches Molly tear open the envelope and pull out a piece of paper. It's that real heavy stuff they use for making signs and stuff.

She reads, "Good for one installation, free parts and labor, no expiration date."

She looks over at Nancy. "What is this?"

Tiny laughs. "It'd be easier if I explain it, Molly, since I'll be the one doing the installation.

"We were talking to Mark a little while back and he told us about looking around for a car, and how it was going to be crazy expensive and how you were just going to give up on it. He had done some asking around and got the same answer. Thirty grand or more for a modified car.

"Well, Nancy and me, mostly Nancy, did some more checking, and it turns out that there's two categories. Modified driving and adaptive driving. Modified is real expensive, like thirty or forty thousand, but it's not what you need.

"Since you can use your arms, what you need is adaptive driving, which is a kit that you can buy on the internet and install on pretty much any car."

Molly starts crying, not quiet like she's done earlier tonight, but just bawling. Tiny is having a little trouble going on himself, but he finally says, "So when y'all get a second car, you just let me know, and we'll get it fixed up with hand controls."

I look over at Sylvia. She's sitting there with her

mouth wide open.

I catch Tiny's eye and he grins at me. "I told you when you insisted on me taking that rifle that I was going to have to do something big for you. Turns out it's for Molly instead."

"I don't know what to say, man," I'm damned near in tears myself.

Tiny points to Raymond. "You ain't heard nothing yet."

Raymond stands and motions for Charlotte to join him. They look awful pleased with themselves, and I wonder what's going on.

"I felt a connection with this young man from the first," Raymond says, and Charlotte nods. "He has a sense of himself that is rare for anyone, and especially for one so young."

Charlotte breaks in. "I think he was a little jealous of Boone just traveling around with Frankie until I reminded him that's essentially what we do as well."

"At any rate, I was so pleased when he called me some months ago and asked if he could come visit and bring someone with him." He gestures to Molly. "As I have said to Boone on a number of occasions, you are an extraordinary young woman, and the two of you are connected in a way that few people achieve."

I lean over to Molly. "He always sounds like he's

giving some kind of speech." She jabs me in the side and says, "Shhhh!"

Tiny hands Raymond an envelope.

"The visit went so well that Charlotte and I began thinking about the estate. Certainly some work was needed on the house, and is in process as we speak, because it was not accessible for one of our guests."

"I do feel bad about that," says Charlotte. We were unintentionally insensitive, but we are working to remedy that."

"Indeed. We have plans to add some walking trails to our property and have asked Molly to consult with us in order to make at least some of them wheelchair accessible.

"But that is not what this is about," he waves the envelope in the air. "We have fifty acres of beautiful land in the middle of the Shenandoah Valley, and Charlotte and I have decided that forty-nine is sufficient for us."

He hands me the envelope. "This is a deed to one acre of land on our property. You may choose the site."

"Within limits," says Charlotte. She looks at Molly. "The one acre cannot include the library, dear. I'm sorry."

Molly bursts out laughing.

"Or the wine cellar," says Raymond, "or the billiard room or, in fact, any part of the main house.

You may wish to wait until the weather turns to return to the estate and choose your acre."

I grin at him, trying to keep from crying right there in front of everybody. "I think so. If we're going to be pitching a tent while we decide what to to with the land, I think waiting until spring is a pretty good idea."

Raymond matches my grin. "I encourage you to think about the conditions of the gift, my friend. I specifically said the acre cannot include the main house."

Chapter Thirty-Three

The day between the party and the wedding goes by in a flash.

Molly and I meet Frances, Momma, Rikki, Hannah, and Mrs. Cooperton for lunch at a burger place we like, partly because they're set up for Molly to get around pretty easy.

At first it's a good lunch. I haven't seen Hannah in a while, and having her and Momma and Frances all here at once is like having my old family back together, except better since Daddy's not here.

"Wow, Boone, you got some really great stuff last night," says Hannah. "Better than Christmas, even."

Frances laughs. "I'm sure when it comes time for you to get married you'll get some really great stuff, too, dear."

Hannah looks at Momma. "How come you look so sad, Momma?"

Rikki touches her on the arm and Momma says, "What?" Rikki tilts her head toward Hannah.

"You look sad," Hannah says. "Are you sad?"

Momma shakes her head. "I'm fine, baby. I guess I'm a little tired."

She looks over at Rikki. "Why don't we go on back to the motel? I might like to lay down for a little bit."

Next thing I know they're gone, and the rest of us are sitting around the table staring at each other.

"What just happened?" I look at Molly, but before she can say anything Frances says, "I think it's what I said, Boone."

I still don't get it, but a lot of the time I don't get this kind of thing.

Molly says, "Sweetie, I think your mother is realizing how much she's missed out on."

Frances nods. "Exactly. She hasn't had any real contact with the two of you for years. You have turned into a young man, and a fine one at that, and my comment about Hannah getting married someday emphasized that her children are almost grown."

"I don't want her to be sad, though," says Hannah. "Maybe I'll tell her it'll be a long time before I get married. I don't even have a boyfriend."

"And I'm very glad of that," says Mrs. Cooperton. "I have enough to do with you and Sam and, I don't think I've told you this yet, we have another foster child coming in two weeks. I'll have my hands full without worrying about boyfriends. I think your mother knows it's going to be a while before you're old enough to even think about marriage, but my guess is she's looking at the lost time she can never get back."

Poor Momma. She can't find a way to be happy, I guess. It's always going to be something.

"I'm still hungry," says Frances after a minute. "Anyone up for dessert?"

We had kept back one menu since none of the other folks have been here before, but Molly and I always split the lava cake. It's too much chocolate even for me, but it's about right for the two of us.

When everybody's ordered and the waitress is gone, Mrs. Cooperton turns to Molly. "So, what are your plans for a honeymoon?"

Damn, I think, I never even thought about that. We should have talked about where we want to go before now. Molly squeezes my leg and says, "You know, we've been so caught up in all the planning and everything, neither one of us has even thought about a honeymoon. Unless you've got some ideas I don't know about," and she grins at me.

I shake my head. "Hell, I don't even know what I'm going to say tomorrow," but when I see the look on her face I say, "I'm kidding. I've got three or four speeches all written out and ready to go. I figure I'll put them all in a hat and pull one out on the way to the ceremony."

"Don't you dare tease her like that, Boone," says

Frances. "She's been working twenty-four hours a day on this, and you've had one job."

The truth is, I don't know what I'm going to say. I've got a thing written out and every time I look at it I think, that's the stupidest thing I've ever seen. I really want to get this right, and I'm scared as hell I'll blow it and ruin her wedding.

Molly says, "It'll be fine, sweetie, really. I can tell you're really stressing out about this and I can promise you I'll love whatever you say."

She doesn't know how lame this thing is I've written.

First I tried to remember stuff from movies, but I don't watch that kind of movie much. All I can think of is stuff like love everlasting and you are the sun and moon and all that, and none of it sounds like me. None of it. I'll use it if I have to, but I'm going to feel like a damn fool saying this stuff.

Molly pokes me and I realize Hannah's asking me something.

"I said, are you going to move to Virginia? That Raymond guy just gave you a whole acre of land. I'd move if I was you."

I'm thinking, if Hannah goes back to Middle Tennessee, and Frances does, too, and Momma goes back to Chicago or wherever, and Sylvia moves to The Commons, Virginia might not be too bad.

"Well, you know, we don't know anybody in

Virginia except Raymond and Charlotte, and it's just a piece of land."

"You could camp out. It'd be great. Oh," she looks at Molly, "can you camp? I mean, you being in a wheelchair."

"I have never tried camping since I got my chair," says Molly, "but I could try it. What do you think, sweetie?"

Hannah says, "Is it weird, like, not being able to walk or anything? I think it'd be really weird."

"Hannah!" Mrs. Cooperton says. She sounds real mad. "You apologize right now!"

Molly jumps in. "It's okay, Mrs. Cooperton, it really is. It's a legitimate question, and what feels weird to me is, I can tell people are wondering the same thing as Hannah, they just won't come out and ask the question."

She turns to Hannah. "Yes. It is. Weird. And sometimes it really pisses me off. Don't tell Gram I said that, okay? She thinks it's unladylike to use crude language."

Hannah nods.

"It makes a big difference that most people are really good about helping me when I need it. Your brother helps me in and out of his truck because it's too high for me to just grab hold and pull myself in. Remember that first time, sweetie? You were standing there not knowing what to do and I said,

'Just pick me up,' and you were so worried you were going to do something wrong or drop me or whatever.

"Most of the things that are different I've got figured out, like finding this place. This restaurant has enough room between the tables for me to get around, and that's better than some places."

"There's places we can't go," I say, "and what I think is, if they won't fix it so Molly can go there, it's no place I want to be anyway."

Molly studies Hannah's face and smiles, then laughs out loud. "You're wondering how me and your brother fool around, aren't you?"

Hannah's face gets beet red and she won't look at Molly.

"Well, I'll tell you," says Molly, and she leans toward Hannah. "I'm looking forward to figuring that out, because I love your brother a lot. I probably won't tell you much more than that even after we're married."

"I think we should change the subject," says Frances. "Some things need to stay private. Don't you agree, Hannah?"

"I guess so."

I can tell she wants to keep on talking about this, but she knows it's not going to happen.

"I will tell you this," Molly says, looking right at Hannah. "There's a lot about being in a chair that is weird, and awkward, and takes some extra work to figure things out. But, your brother told me once that if he was thinking about marrying somebody he sure wouldn't let something like a wheelchair get in the way. I just love that, don't you?"

Chapter Thirty-Four

Mark looks at the people gathered in the living room. "I've been looking forward to this day for a very long time." He turns to me. "Ready, Boone?"

I nod. "If I look like I'm going to pass out or something, talk faster."

He laughs. "You've got it."

He turns to face the crowd. "Good morning, everyone. Today is a very good day, and it's about to get even better." He looks down at Molly. "Ready?"

She nods.

"All right, then." He switches to his preacher's voice and raises his head. "Family and friends of this fine young couple, we are all here . . . ."

I'm looking at Molly and thinking she's the most beautiful thing I've ever seen and I must have missed some stuff because the next thing I hear Mark say is, "Boone and Molly have some things they would like to say to each other. Boone, why don't you go first?"

Here it is. I've been scared lots of times in my life,

but this is about at the top of the list. I take a deep breath and look into Molly's eyes. Right then I forget everything I had planned to say, and I just start talking.

"I remember when I got a phone call about clearing out some rose bushes, I guess a year and a half ago. I found the house and knocked, and I was expecting an old woman. No offense, Sylvia," and I grin at her.

"None taken," she says, and everybody laughs.

"So when the door opened and it was you I was real surprised.

"I knew right off you were pretty, and it didn't take me long to figure out you're smart and funny, too, and you don't take any stuff off of anybody. Pretty soon I was thinking about you all the time. I wasn't really planning to propose there in Mark's office. Maybe I figured if you said no I'd have him right there to put me back together again. That's about as scared as I've ever been, except for right now, and I'm real glad you said yes. I don't have a whole lot to offer, but whatever I've got is yours now. I can't even think about not being with you." I stop for a second and turn to Mark. "I guess that's it."

Mark nods. "Well said, Boone. Molly, it's your turn."

Molly is quiet for a minute.

"When I opened the door and saw a really good-looking guy standing there, I thought he'd either ignore me or just see a cripple. You didn't do either one.

"I could tell right away that you really saw me, and I wasn't sure what to do about that. That time after you finished with Gram's roses, when I asked you out, that was the first time in a very long time I had done anything like that. Boy, am I glad I did. It was easy with you, Boone, right from the first.

"Then at the basketball court, when you stood up for me without picking a fight about it, that was just beautiful. Like a real man."

It feels like she's talking to me and to Momma at the same time, but I don't look away to see how Momma is taking it. I can't look anywhere else.

"You're a better man than you think you are, and I just love that about you. In fact, I love everything about you, and I can't wait to get this ceremony over with so it'll be official and I'll know I'm not making all this up. I worry about that, you know? That it's too good? So let's wrap this up so I'll know it's real."

She turns to Mark. "Okay?"

He nods. "Okay." He looks at Tiny. "I assume you have the rings?"

"Just one," he says. "One of them's got the other one." He points to Nancy and Charlotte.

I knew Molly was having trouble deciding which one to ask to be up here with her, and I guess she decided to ask both of them.

"Have you seen these, Mark?" Tiny says. Mark shakes his head. "Man, these things are beautiful. They're going to knock you right on your, I mean, you're really going to be impressed." He shrugs. "Almost messed up there. This best man stuff is harder than it looks."

He hands me Molly's ring, and when I look at Molly she has mine in her hand.

Mark whistles. "Someone has excellent taste."

I got to say they look good.

He goes through some stuff that I have to repeat after him, about love and honor and sticking with each other. Molly has to do the same thing, and at the end she smiles at Mark. "Nice job."

He bows his head a little. "Thanks. I just took the traditional passage and played with it a little bit." He looks at me.

"Boone, it's time for Molly to start wearing her ring."

I figure that's my cue, and I start to put the ring on and stop. "Where's the other ring? The one I gave you already?"

"The wedding ring goes closest to the heart," Mark says. "She'll put the other one back on later."

Damn, there's a lot I don't know. I slide the ring on and say, "I love you, Molly." Don't know if that's supposed to be part of this, but I say it anyway.

"I know," she says, "me, too."

She slides on my ring, and Mark says, "Okay, it's official. Molly, you may kiss your groom."

Molly laughs out loud and says, "Thank you for that, Mark," and pulls me down into a kiss that is pretty short but real intense.

Everybody starts clapping and shouting, and Mark says, "Go on, be with all these people that love you so much. I'll have the paperwork for you later. And, just so you know, I will be deeply insulted if either of you tries to pay me for this."

We don't actually go anywhere. Everybody comes up to us, and I see Raymond go up to Mark and shake his hand.

Molly's mother is bent over whispering in her ear, and I try to think of her name. Regina, I'm pretty sure, but she doesn't go by that. I see her straighten up and come towards me and just before she gets here I think, Ginny. Maybe it's Ginny.

"Boone, I just want to say thank you for making my daughter so happy. I haven't seen her like this since before, before her accident."

"Ma'am, it works both ways. She's the best thing that ever happened to me, no doubt about it."

She shakes a finger at me. "None of this ma'am stuff. It's Ginny, and I'm so glad you're going to be part of the family." She grabs me and starts hugging me, and I'll be damned if she doesn't start crying.

"Sorry," she says when she finally lets go. "I've got makeup all over your beautiful white shirt. I just was so afraid that no one else would see what I see when I look at her."

"Ma'am, I mean Ginny, I don't know about anybody else, and to tell you the truth, I don't much care what they think. I know how great she is."

She nods. "Right. Absolutely right."

I don't even see Momma coming up, but all of a sudden she's right there beside us.

"Hello, Natalie," Ginny says. "You raised a fine young man here."

Momma looks like she doesn't know what to say, but after a minute she says, "Thank you. He's a good boy."

I'm waiting for her to say something nice about Molly, but she just stands there, and after a minute Ginny says, "I think I'm going to go talk to Sylvia."

She walks away and Momma says, "What did you tell her about me?"

"Nothing, Momma. I just met her when she came down for the wedding."

"Sounded like she was making fun of me. Does she know you've been raising yourself the last five years?"

I shake my head. "She doesn't know anything about that, Momma. She was just trying to be nice."

She's quiet for a minute. "Anyway, I just came

over to tell you goodbye. Rikki and I are going back to the motel, and we're going to get an early start tomorrow. It's a long drive."

The first thing I think is, why is she doing this? She's taking the best day of my life and pissing all over it. I feel like I ought to be getting mad at her, but I can't find it in me. All I feel right now is sorry for her, and, to tell the truth, if this is how she's going to be I'm glad she's leaving.

"Let me find Hannah and we'll walk you out to the car."

She shakes her head. "I can't stand it, son. I just can't. I got to go now."

She turns and walks toward the front door. Rikki is already standing there and looks right at me, making motions like she's using her phone. Does that mean she's going to call me, or that I'm supposed to call her? I'm still trying to figure it out when the door closes behind them and they're gone.

Chapter Thirty-Five

Finding a place for our honeymoon that is good for Molly and that will let us bring Frankie isn't easy. Molly says it gets a little better every year, but it still takes a while to decide where to go. We decide on April because of the weather, and also because Molly wants to be here to help Sylvia with the move.

The week leading up to her leaving the house is weird. We're spending most of the time at her house, mainly to keep her from being alone, and I guess Molly's having a little trouble letting go, too.

I'm not working much, just a half a day or a day every now and then, which is good because of Sylvia.

We pick out a room and clear everything out of it, and Sylvia puts stuff in there she's going to take with her. Molly's stuff we're starting to move to my place, so it's pretty much a mess at both houses all the time.

We get Tiny to help with his truck, and with him and my truck and Sylvia's car we get most of her stuff moved in one trip. The place is real nice, and I get why she's okay with moving here. She's not even moved in yet and she knows people, and it looks like to me she's going to be okay. When I tell Molly that she gives me a look and just says, "I hope you're right, sweetie."

I never thought about it, but with Sylvia moving, we sort of have to get Molly a cell phone of her own. So now we're paying for two phones and I can see things getting more expensive right in front of me.

Molly's on her phone a lot after Sylvia moves. She's talking to her four or five times a day, and sometimes when she's done she's all teary and quiet. If I knew a good thing to say I'd sure say it, but I never have been worth a damn at that kind of thing.

It takes a while to sell the house, I guess because of it being winter, but that gives us more time to clear out all the stuff, and there's a bunch. I've seen worse. Some of the jobs I've done have been just awful, but there is a lot here, for sure.

Tiny is over one time helping get stuff organized for another sale and asks about buying the place for him and Nancy, but when I tell him what they're asking for it he laughs that short laugh of his and says, "Guess not."

"How is she?"

"Not quite about to pop, but we're still a while away. The doc is saying early spring. I mean, he gave her an exact date, but neither one of us is putting much stock in that. He'll get here when he's good and ready."

"You gonna have a boy?"

He shrugs. "Nancy and her mom say they can tell. We haven't had any tests done or anything, so who knows?"

I didn't know Nancy and her mom were doing okay. When I ask about that, Tiny says, "They're good, but Stan's a whole different thing. That man can carry a grudge like nobody I've ever seen, and his son's about the same."

"I've met his son. Cyrus is a piece of work, all right."

He gives me a look. "Stan still blames you for this, you know, corrupting his little girl and all that, and Cyrus is right with him. If I were you, I'd try not to run into them on a back road anywhere."

"I got no reason to go around there. Long as they don't try to track me down I figure I'm okay."

I think about the last couple of times I've seen Betty at the home and the way she's treated me, and I know that's how this kind of shit gets started. A guy can get a reputation just because a couple of people decide he's done something they don't like, and it doesn't make a damn bit of difference if it's true or not.

When I tell Molly all this she nods. "I talk to Nancy once in a while, and she's told me pretty much the same thing. Guess they can't really get mad at Tiny, since he stepped up and married her and all, and they sure can't blame Nancy. You're easy, sweetie. You're not even around. They can badmouth you all they want and there's nobody to stand up for you."

I almost say I wish Tiny would, but I know better than that. He's got to live right in the middle of all that.

For a while right after the wedding I thought Sylvia was going to give us her car, since Molly got that gift from Tiny at the wedding. She found out that some of the folks at The Commons had cars, though, and decided to hang on to hers.

"Just for a little while, dear," she had said to Molly. "I'll probably find out it's more trouble than it's worth."

I've got Tiny looking around for a deal just in case a little while turns into a long one. He's a lot better at that than I'll ever be, and if he finds one that he says is good, I'm not going to worry about it. It'll be in good shape, for sure, and he can just do the hand control kit as soon as we close the deal.

"I don't want to wait even a day, but I know I need to," says Molly after I get a call from Tiny about one he thought was going to be a good one. It turns out it had a leaking head gasket, which I guess is a big deal, and Tiny just walked away from it.

"He'll find you a good one," I say.

"I know. I'm just anxious. You have no idea how much I want to be able to come and go on my own."

The real estate guy wants the home to be open any time, and says we should not be living there unless we're willing to keep it looking like nobody lives there in case somebody wants to come see it.

"I can't sell a place with dirty dishes in the sink and dog hair all over the place," he says, and I guess I see that. So Molly is pretty much moved in with me and Frankie. Bert and Ray are at The Commons with Sylvia, and the old place is empty.

"He needs to sell it soon," Molly says. We're having a cup of coffee and making plans for our trip. She's decided she wants to see the ocean, so we're looking for a place that has a boardwalk out on the beach and will let us take Frankie out with us. We can get a place to stay that will allow us to have a dog, but we might have to lie about how big Frankie is. I got no problem with doing that.

"He will," I say. "It's a nice place, and it has a few acres with it. Soon as the weather warms up a little bit."

We finally settle on Carolina Beach, and it's a lot different than the last time I went to see the Atlantic Ocean. Molly does a lot of research, so we know we're going to a place that is accessible for her, and that allows pets in a lot of places. I got to say this time I'm enjoying myself a lot more than the last time. We spend four days there and might go back again sometime. There's a bunch of stuff we don't get to.

I still like mountains better.

On the way back Molly says, "I talked to your mother a little while back."

I almost drive out of my lane. "How the hell did she get your number?"

"Well, you know, Mark has both our numbers, and I think she called him to get it."

"Why didn't she call me?"

"I think she feels bad about how she just took off at the wedding. She's trying, Boone, she really is, but it feels like right now she's afraid she can't talk to either one of us without saying the wrong thing."

I don't say anything.

It kind of feels that way to me, too. My memory of Momma before Frankie died is getting so faint I can barely see her. After that she was so beat down it was like she wasn't there at all. Now it's like she's right on the edge of being mad pretty much all the time, and it sneaks up on her when she doesn't even know it's coming.

I guess I understand that.

"I had a phone call the other day, too," I say.

"Who from?"

"Corey."

"Did you have to turn down a job because of our

honeymoon?"

I shake my head. "I won't be doing any more work for Corey."

"What happened?"

"I don't know how much money he got in that inheritance, but he's decided not to keep going with the whole recreate the town from a hundred years ago thing."

"So why did he call you?"

I laugh. "He wanted to know what I knew about beekeeping. That big field behind the building, where he was going to put in houses and streets and all that shit, you know?"

"Right," she says.

"He's got two dozen hives, and he's going to plant the whole field in wildflowers. Going into the honey business, I guess."

"So you aren't going into the honey business with him?"

I think about Trevor's mom and shake my head. "No way am I spending that much time around anything that can sting me."

"What about all those barns you cleared out? I know there must have been a swarm once in a while."

"There was, but if somebody had tried to hire me to clear out two dozen swarms of bees, I'd have turned him down flat."

Molly runs her hand up and down my thigh. "I

knew you were smart the first time we met. That's why I married you, you know."

I grin at her. "And here I thought it was just for the sex."

"Well, yeah. That, too."

Chapter Thirty-Six

Me and Molly and Frankie are on our way up to Raymond and Charlotte's place. They're not there right now, somewhere up in Minnesota I think, but Raymond said to go have a look around.

"He told me to remember the conditions of the gift," I say. "He made a big deal about that when he gave it to us."

"I remember."

"He said he left us a map of the property in the cabin with the part we can't choose from marked in red."

"He's got something in mind, doesn't he?"

I nod. "He always does. He's got real close to Mark, did you know that?"

"Really?" Molly says. After a second she says, "Actually, I can see that. They would appreciate each other, I think. How did you know? Did Mark tell you?"

"No," I say. "Raymond did. He's trying to talk

Mark into looking for a new job."

"Really?" Molly says again. "Why?"

"According to Raymond, Mark is too good to do the kind of work he's doing at the home. He needs to get out of there.

"He says it a lot fancier than that, you know. I mean, Raymond doesn't pass up a chance to give a little speech even if he's just talking to one person. He thinks Mark should be like a hospital chaplain and not just be around people who are getting ready to die. He should do stuff for people who are going to get better."

"I don't know about that," says Molly. "What does Mark think about it?"

I shrug. "Haven't talked to Mark, just Raymond. He's got a friend, somebody who's a big deal in a hospital up in Virginia somewhere, and he says he's going to tell him about Mark."

We're driving along and I'm thinking, if Mark does do this hospital thing, that's one less reason for me and Molly to stay where we are. The house sold a month ago, so we don't have to worry about that. Sylvia's already practically in Virginia, Hannah and Frances are both in Middle Tennessee, and Momma's up around Chicago some place. Tiny and Nancy are still living back down where I grew up, and I got no reason to go back there except to see them. The kind of work I do I can do anywhere.

We pull into Raymond and Charlotte's driveway and park close to the little cabin. It's a real pretty place, right there on the pond, and I'm glad to be back up here.

I open the door and Frankie jumps down to the ground. She heads toward the main house, sniffs around the back patio, and trots down to the cabin. I'm watching her go and thinking how big a deal Raymond made of this acre they gave us not including the main house, and how he didn't say a word about the cabin.

I get Molly's chair and she settles in, and we start down the path. I start to say something to her about what I was just thinking when she says, "You know, sweetie, all the time Raymond was talking about where we could choose our piece of land, he never once said the cabin was off limits. Just the main house. He made a big point of the main house and, you know, I believe that he was deliberately not mentioning the cabin."

"I was thinking the same thing."

We get to the cabin and stop on the front porch. The afternoon sun is hitting the pond, and there's all kinds of movement in the water. Everything's starting to wake up for the spring season, and the splashing of the water is about the only thing we can hear.

We both get real still and let it be quiet all around

us, and I bet it's five minutes before either one of us moves.

"Sweetie?"

I don't say anything, and she reaches over and takes my hand. "Let's go in and take a look at the map Raymond left us."

I say okay, but I'm not sure I need to look at any map. We go inside and there's a map on the kitchen table, just like he said there would be, and it's already unrolled. There's a salt shaker holding down one corner and a couple of books holding down the other side. The fourth corner is kind of curled up a little bit.

I start toward the table and Molly stops me. "Boone."

She's still at the door, and it's a few seconds before I see what she sees.

The stove is on the opposite wall, and the counter runs along it just like before. Except now, to the right of the stove the counter is about six or seven inches lower than it was and there's room for Molly to roll up underneath it. The sink is on the same level and set up the same way, and it's like the whole counter from the stove all the way to the end is designed just for her.

She rolls over to the counter and up underneath it, rests her hands on the surface, and leans forward to the knife rack at the back. She doesn't pull one out, just touches it and backs up, does a little back and forth until she's facing the sink, and makes sure she can reach the faucets.

The counter ends at the back door, and next to it on the right wall is a bookcase that I'm pretty sure wasn't there before. There are two or three books propped up on the middle shelf, but it's mostly empty, and there's a skylight that's also new. The corner is just what a reader like Molly would love.

"I wonder what else he's had done," I say, but she's not paying any attention to me. She's already over at the bookcase corner.

"I could definitely live here." It's a low whisper, so soft that if I hadn't come up behind her I'd never have heard it.

I start to say something, but decide not to and move over to the table where the map is. Sure enough, the main house and the area just around it are shaded in red. There's some writing in a few places with arrows, and it looks like he's thinking about the trails he had talked about when we were up here for those two weeks.

I can tell from the map most of their land is woods, and there's a couple of streams and another pond back toward the opposite boundary. I'd love to check out the whole place with Frankie, but Molly couldn't go with us.

"You and Frankie should check out the rest of the

property just in case," says Molly, "but I know which acre I want us to have."

I hadn't heard her come up next to me.

"I was wondering what the rest of the place is like," I say, and she nods.

"I could tell. How long are Raymond and Charlotte going to be gone?"

I shrug. "Who knows? Lots of the time they don't even know themselves."

"Why don't we settle in here and you two spend the next few days looking the property over?"

"We could do that." I look at the map again and then back at her. "I love you a lot, you know."

"I know."

"I like this cabin. Feels like home."

She nods. "To me, too."

She points to the books on the table and in the bookcase. "I bet Charlotte picked those out for me so I'll have something to read while you two are out exploring."

I look around the cabin. It's not near as big as Gamaliel's old place but it's in a lot better shape. The kitchen and the table where the map is laid out are sort of part of the living room, and there's a short hall with a couple of bedrooms and a bathroom. That's all there is, but it's enough. Plenty for me and Molly and Frankie. I realize that in my head I've already made up my mind. It feels like I'm finally letting go of a whole big chunk of my life, and I'm not even a little sorry to see it gone. I've been needing to do this for a while now, I think.

"About damn time," I say, real soft.

"It sure is," Molly says with a smile. "Welcome home, sweetie."

End of Book Six

This Concludes the Boone Series

Afterword

When I began *Pushing Back* as a NaNoWriMo project, I didn't know it would turn into a six book series. Working with teenagers on the fringes of society indirectly led to the creation of Boone, and as he told me more of his story, it started to make sense to create a series of books about an Appalachian teen coming of age more or less on his own.

My career in education focused almost exclusively on teens in treatment centers and residential facilities. These children, the ones I spent much of my professional career teaching and learning from, are marginalized, stereotyped, and ignored, unless they do or say something that supports society's negative assumptions about them. As with most groups who suffer from this kind of prejudice, these young people are more like us than not, and I have been pleased to offer Boone a chance to tell his story. I was deliberately vague about the locations in the series; I see Boone as a teenage Everyman whose experiences, trials, failures, and successes are a distillation of the hundreds of young people I worked with over the years.

There's a little of me in Boone, of course. I would be foolish to deny that. We both hail from East Tennessee. I grew up in a rural area, got an extra helping when they were passing out insecurity, and am generally uncomfortable in crowds, much like Boone. Beyond that our paths diverge pretty sharply; I was well raised, my birth family stayed intact until the deaths of my parents well into my late sixties, and I both valued and enjoyed the formal education system. Boone is his own man, no question.

Here, at the end of the series, many people are due thanks and recognition: my wife Suzanne (first reader extraordinaire), my fellow authors at the Author's Guild of Tennessee, Joel Simmons for his help with Molly's character, my friend Jim for our ongoing conversations about the series, Tilmer, Sandy, and Annie for their insightful essays in the box set *Stumbling Into Adulthood*, Nick Castle for a beautiful set of covers, and the readers who sent emails or sought me out at craft fairs and festivals to tell me how much they were enjoying the series. I'm sure this could be a much longer list. My apologies to those I am failing to mention; your contributions are not lessened because of my faulty memory.

Most of all, my thanks to the young people I had the privilege to know over the years. You taught me as much as I taught you, and I appreciate your allowing me to see beyond the stereotypes to the fine individuals you are. You are stronger, braver, and smarter than you are given credit for being. Remember that. Act on that knowledge.